Turbulent Passion

Turbulent Passion

The Flyboy Series

G.L. Ross

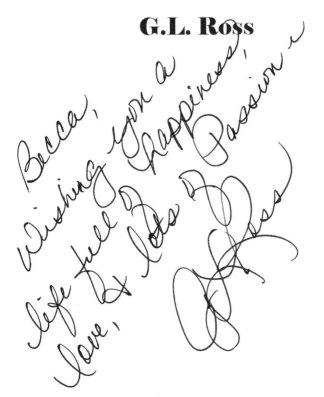

This book is a work of fiction. Any references to real people, businesses, restaurants, airlines, airports, places, and names are used fictitiously. Other names, characters, places, businesses, restaurants, airlines, airports, and events are products of the author's imagination. Any resemblances are entirely coincidental.

All rights reserved. No part of this book may be reproduced, scanned, or distributed in any printed or electronic form without permission. Please purchase only authorized editions.

First Printing, February 2014

Copyright © 2013 by Gayle L. Ross

All Rights Reserved

The Cataloging-in-Publication Data is on file at Library of Congress

Printed in the United States of America

ISBN: 978-1495347849

Cover design by James GoOnWrite.com

This book is dedicated to all the men who affected my life, whether in a good, bad, or ugly way. You made me the woman I am today.

Acknowledgments

Years ago I dreamt of writing a novel. Many times I attempted to put thought to print, but something always got in the way. I finally decided 2013 was the year I would complete my first romantic manuscript. This goal would not have been reached without the assistance of Lisa Renee Jones; Lisa, thank you for encouraging me, answering my numerous questions, and guiding me through the transition of children's author to adult contemporary author and the "indie" world. I wish you and Diego a lifetime of happiness! If you haven't read one of Lisa's books please do – you will not be disappointed.

I would also like to thank my "beta test readers," Lucy, Paula, and Haley. You ladies sent me to the moon and back with your reactions and comments. Also, a huge thank-you to my website designer, Robert Ross; you are a tremendous brother and computer guru. The last thank you is to my son, Brandon. Thanks for putting up with Mom's "silence is golden" attitude when "in the zone." *Oh and by the way, "No, you still cannot be a test reader."*

Thank you for reading the first book in the *Flyboy* series. I hope you laughed, cried, and fell in love with Lisa & Lance. To those who have blogged, reviewed, tweeted, and texted about *Turbulent Passion* – THANK YOU! Please continue to spread the word. I encourage all of you to check out the songs and musical artists mentioned in the book. I am heading "back to the zone" now, to complete *Burning Desire*. God Bless & Keep Reading!

Turbulent Passion

Turbulent Passion

Chapter One

Lance

Every night I see her in my dreams. Honestly, I can't remember a single night I didn't dream of her. Her mesmerizing emerald green eyes began haunting me in my early teens. I would wake from a wet dream, with her eyes penetrating my thoughts and desires. For years, I searched for her in malls, movie theatres, at sporting events, but to no avail. Eventually, I surrendered my hopes and dreams of finding the "green-eyed goddess" and began screwing every brick-house blond I could find. I relentlessly tried to erase and escape the memories of the goddesses' long blond hair, her perfect petite body with sculpted tits and perky nipples, and the way my hands fit perfectly around her tiny, tempting, curvy waist. But, damn it, I can't forget her alluring smile as she wraps her toned legs around my waist and lowers onto my hard, pulsing dick. We fit – together – perfectly. Her green eyes turn black as our ride delves deeper and I push her toward her second scream worthy orgasm. Her creamy, sweet, ivory skin drives me wild, especially her soft, silky neck, which is completely exposed when her head drops

G.L. Ross

back as she cums. My tongue traces and teases her every nook and cranny until I can no longer resist biting her gorgeous, plump bottom lip. Her eyes flash open wide in response. Hunger radiates in her eyes. *We never get enough of each other.* She makes me feel things I never imagined possible. I never thought I could desire one person twenty-four hours a day, but I do. *Who is this green eyed goddess?*

Trust me, I realize she is a fantasy, but even after twenty years, every single, testosterone filled day, I continue my search for her, in airport terminals and hotel lobbies. Hell, what would I do if I found her? Attack and grope her? Sure, I can see it now, "You don't know me but we have hot, mind blowing sex together. We have for twenty years." That would go over well…Not!

I need a cold shower, along with a reality check. Wonder if I have a curvy blond on tonight's flight attendant crew? Someone to bury myself in while I close my eyes and imagine those gorgeous, green eyes glazing over as I palm her firm, full breast, while rubbing my thumb over her erect nipple. *Damn! I am obsessed!*

Turbulent Passion

Lisa

Maybe I'll go to graduate school. I could become a psychologist; all my friends think I am their twenty-four hour on-call shrink anyway.

Maryanne rang me at two thirty this morning. Woke me up to cry and complain about how Matt had broken her heart. "He is so unromantic. It is our one year anniversary and he takes me to an action flick. An action flick, can you believe that Lisa? Then he wants to go do it in the back of his car, really? I mean really?" I wait to make sure she is *really* finished. *Maryanne asks numerous questions, but doesn't actually want you to respond, to any of them.* She merely wants to vent to the Universe.

"Maryanne, has Matt ever done anything you wanted to do the entire time you've been seeing him? No, he hasn't." This time I won't allow her time to answer *my* question. *Yes, I am annoyed.* She woke me up to complain about Matt's, unfortunately, normal behavior, which she chooses to put up with on a daily basis. There's absolutely no need for her to answer the question or make excuses for him or herself.

G.L. Ross

"But, Lisa he loves me. I know he does."
Blah, blah, blah.

I bury my head under my large, fluffy pillow. "Okay, let's say he does, just for grins sake, but does he respect you? Obviously not, so move on and find someone who deserves you and cares about your feelings. Men need to treat women with respect and love. Never settle for less, Maryanne."

"Lisa, you are so strong. I'm not like you. I'm not that strong, plus I get lonely. I don't know what I would do without Matt. I can't go without someone, like you do." *Thanks for reminding me.*

Frustration builds as I roll onto my back; turning my head I stare at the time on the alarm clock. "Maryanne, Maryanne," I condescendingly mutter. "Go see Matt later today and tell him how he made you feel. Now, please, for the love of Pete, get some sleep. Good night - good morning - good whatever the hell time of day it is."

"Night, Lisa. I love you, thanks for listening."

Turbulent Passion

I can't help but moan while dropping the phone back on my bedside table. *Why is it women allow themselves to be treated disrespectfully?* I would rather be alone then be with someone like Matt.

"Anyway, back to present day and today's mission. Graduate school in psychology might work. I could even find a part time job while going to classes or work during the day and classes at night. Of course I'd better get busy applying to universities *today*, it may be too late to apply and receive acceptance." *Why am I speaking out loud to myself?* I really need to get a life *and soon.*

I locate the graduate school application site for The University of Texas at Dallas. "Let's see, age? Twenty-three." Yes, I took the five year plan through college. I changed degrees three times and dropped classes due to late night partying causing oversleeping of 8:00 AM classes. Why would anyone want to teach an 8:00 AM class? *Ugh, painful memory.*

"What?" I respond to an unexpected knock at my door, "Who could that be?" Speaking to the air,

G.L. Ross

again, Lisa. You really need to stop talking to yourself.

My vibrant friend, Lucy, greets me at the door. Lucy is really short, petite, and a bundle full of energy. We met doing volunteer work last summer at the animal shelter. We weren't much help though, because we wanted to play with all of the animals rather than clean their cages.

"Hey girl, what are you doing?"

Lucy pats me on the face and heads into my den while extending a backwards compliment, "Oh, Miss Lisa. You are so pretty, even without your make up." *That's my Lucy.* She knows I hate wearing make-up, especially when at home. I figure I'm not going anywhere to try and impress anyone, so why hassle with it. Lucy, on the other hand, always looks perfect and doesn't know or understand the true meaning of dressing casual. If she runs to the grocery store she has full make-up and hair. She's a flight attendant for International Air and seems to think she is always on a plane; crisp and perfect all the frickin' time.

Turbulent Passion

"Lisa, I've had a fabulous idea, so you need to dig out a picture of you smiling and with make-up; a color one that shows off those magnificent green eyes."

I climb into my oversized yellow chair, tucking my legs under my tush. "Lucy, please have a seat and why do you need my picture?"

Lucy chooses to sit on the edge of my robin egg blue sofa, crossing her ankles, *again so prim and proper*. "You, my dear, are filling out an application to be a flight attendant, with me! Isn't that great?" She exuberantly declares.

"I can't be a flight attendant. I don't even like flying. My ears hurt and I absolutely hate heights."

Flashing her dynamic, "hello – good-bye," smile she attempts to convince me, "It will be fine. When you are talking to passengers your ears stay open and you never have time to look out the window, so you will have no idea how high you are."

I attempt an explanation, "I was filling out an application for grad school when you knocked on the door. I've decided to get my masters in psychology. I'm going to get paid for all of my late night counseling." *That should appease her*…maybe.

"That is terrific Lisa, but you can still fly." Why did I know she would say that? "You will fly on the weekends and go to class during the week. You can even study on your overnights, it is perfect. Now get me that picture." *So much for appeasing her.*

Chapter Two

Possessed

Yesterday, I discovered a woman who from a rear view was shaped like *my* goddess. Her hair was even styled the same. I'm not sure what possessed me, but I chased her down the terminal. Like a complete and total idiot, I grabbed her arm, which completely freaked her out. She spun around staring at me with puzzled and alarmed *blue* eyes. Yes, damn it, blue eyes. I attempted to apologize and explain my confusion, but hell I don't understand my ridiculous, obsessed actions.

I am possessed by an imaginary, dream inspired, woman!

I couldn't even take my DD cupped, young, blond, hard-bodied flight attendant to bed last night. My thoughts were fucking consumed by *the* goddess. Every time I opened or closed my eyes I saw her. I finally told "Miss DD" I wasn't feeling well, rather than her thinking I couldn't get it up. Hell, I could get it up for my green-eyed goddess, just not "Miss DD," even when she's wearing goddesses' imaginary face. *I really am absolutely – mental.*

G.L. Ross

Today, thank goodness, is the dawning of a new day, a day where I will attempt to act like the professional Captain I am, rather than a raging, hormonal teenager. My First Officer and I are hanging in the food court participating in one of my favorite airport activities, people watching. Folks are fascinating. While devouring my double meat, jalapeno and cheese Whataburger, I enjoy studying human behavior.

God has made some beautiful women, *some ugly ones too*, but fortunately our flight attendants are knock-out specimens. Specimens I will gladly take to my hotel bed, except, of course, when my goddess interferes with my fuckin' erection.

There is something about black leather high heeled boots and black dresses that flat turn me on. I think it's the black hose and leather boot combination that gets my juices flowing, especially when the hose are thigh highs. *Yum*. I'm getting hard just thinking about it.

Four of our finest walk by my table laughing. I can't help but admire their legs and curvaceous figures. *Mmm-Mmm*. I recognize the tall,

Turbulent Passion

long legged blond. I think I nailed her on the beach in Maui. As she waves and heads my way, *yep it is her*; I catch a glimpse of a blond in the middle of the harem. My heart jumps and stutters as my imagination once again takes flight. The long legged blond yells to her crew that she will catch up with them later. *What is her name?* The harem turns to wave good-bye and my imagination finally becomes reality and slaps me hard in the face.

Graduate

Lucy, of course, got her way and I submitted my flight attendant application. *Are we really surprised?*

Three weeks after submitting it I attended flight attendant training for International Air, taking tests harder than any I took in college. I was stressed to the max studying all the terms. I swear I trained to be a paramedic, firefighter, and talk show host. I thought I was going to be a flight attendant!

Graduation day arrived quickly and was filled with relief and excitement. Even though my

G.L. Ross

dad feels I am wasting my college education, he was there proudly beaming because I will be earning a paycheck; although he isn't happy that includes paying union dues, being the diehard Republican he is.

"Honey we are so proud of you. Your mom and I are looking forward to using those passes to fly everywhere, free." *"Free" being the key word.*

"Thanks Dad." Dad is always my cheerleader. Then there is Mom. She is happy for me, but also extremely envious of my opportunity to see the world. Mom believes a woman is not complete without a husband, so she constantly scopes for the man *she* feels is my match.

"Now listen to your Mom and have fun. Keep your eyes on high alert. Who knows maybe you will meet the man of your dreams on one of your flights. This job is perfect to meet men, Lisa." My *Mother* is determined I will be married by the age of thirty.

"Mom, I don't have time for a man. I'm going to be studying for my master's degree, plus I'm

Turbulent Passion

not going to settle for just anyone. I want someone who respects and loves me. I want my soul mate."

****

After checking in for our trip, Lucy and I head to gate four. "Lucy, I cannot believe I have been flying for a month now. Time sure does 'fly' by." *Corny joke, but couldn't pass it up.* "How is Scott?" Lucy and Scott have been married five months. Scott is retired Air Force and a Captain for International.

"Married life is wonderful and Scott is my dream come true." She is obviously still in the "honeymoon" stage. "We need to find you a pilot, so we can double date."

Turning to look at Lucy, I raise an eyebrow. "Lucy, you know my number one rule is to never date a pilot."

"Rules are made to be broken," she giggles. *She is such a bad influence.* "Your rule is silly, anyway. There are still good, Christian, single men out there."

G.L. Ross

"Yes, there are, but *they* are not pilots!" I exclaim, before commencing in full blown laughter.

Turbulent Passion

Chapter Three

Captain Miller

Her mesmerizing green eyes danced magically. Her smile lit me up inside like a sparkler, on Memorial Day, *but I froze.* I couldn't speak or move. Completely and totally stunned, I watched her walk away. *My Goddess - I watched walk away, because I was a star-struck idiot.*

I read Alice's name tag, the long legged blond whose name I couldn't remember. *I know. You really don't need to go there. I am a piece of shit. Moving on...new topic.* I ask her where she and her crew are headed. I have to get to the Goddess. She explains they are switching terminals to catch their next flight. I take off after my Goddess as my First Officer hollers after me. Hurrying down the hallway I hit security and Goddess is nowhere to be found. *How could I stand there and let her disappear?* After twenty fucking years of insatiable dreams I *let her* walk away.

I rush back to Alice and inquire about her crew, especially the petite, blond, green-eyed Goddess. I discover she is new, maybe a month on

G.L. Ross

line, Dallas/Fort Worth based, and my Goddess has a name… *Lisa.*

After visiting with Alice, I discover her crew has one more day on their trip and the overnight is on the opposite side of the United States from mine. *Of course!* I ask all types of questions regarding Lisa, *even her name is luscious rolling off my tongue,* especially about her next trip. I completely piss off Alice, but I don't give a damn. *My green-eyed Goddess exists! She really exists and in gorgeous, curvy, silky flesh.*

Naïve Lisa

I love my overnights. The peace and quiet of a hotel room, the crisp, clean sheets, and the endless hot water are a girl's dream, *as far as I am concerned*, especially after ten to twelve hour days on an airplane. I also enjoy sight-seeing, especially with an energetic, petite, brunette friend, who happens to be a full-fledged "energizer bunny" and presently is knocking on my door. *Yes, it is Lucy.*

Turbulent Passion

"You ready? We are going to walk three miles while viewing downtown Philadelphia. I have it all mapped out. Scott was here last week and told me the way to go." *Does she ever breathe? I swear the gal talks faster than my mind computes.*

Lucy is the type of person who plans every minute of every day. Her picture is in the dictionary next to the word "organized."

"Sure, let me grab my key, bottle of water, money, and phone. Yep, I think I have it all, ready or not, let's go."

The square in downtown Philadelphia is really special. The exquisite architecture is a mix of historical and modern, the shops are a nice blend of mom and pop shops and chain stores, and all the couples having picnics, near their row houses, make it the place to be. If the couples are not chasing a toddler then they are playing with their dog. There are big dogs and little dogs everywhere. *How do people keep these big dogs in condominiums and apartments?*

G.L. Ross

Lucy barks at me, "Hey you, where have you wandered off?"

"I was wondering where these people live that have such big dogs," I reply.

"Lisa, you think of the strangest things. Pick up the pace. You're lagging behind." The woman is a drill sergeant.

"By the way Lucy, who was the pilot Alice stayed to talk to in Dallas?"

Lucy thinks for several minutes, before I attempt to describe him, "He had chocolate brown hair and was really tall, muscular, and downright gorgeous." *Yes, I sighed and drooled just now.*

"Ahh…That was Lance - Lance Miller. He's a hound dog."

"A what?" I ask.

"Hound dog. Stay away from him. He will eat you up and spit you out, my dear, naïve, sweet friend."

"I am not naïve," I exclaim.

Turbulent Passion

"Yea, right," Lucy sarcastically remarks. "Trust me. He is not your type, at all."

"Got it, point taken, but he is handsome."

"That he is. Now, back to the important things in life, are you seeing anyone?"

"As in dating?" I breathlessly respond. The girl walks entirely too fast. *How do those short legs carry her so far, so quickly?*

"Yes," she abruptly snaps.

I stop and bend at the waist gasping for air. "Not really. A college friend set me up and that was an absolute nightmare." I gulp water from my bottle before continuing, "A guy from one of my psych classes asked me out, but once again I became a counselor. I heard all about how his girlfriend of four years dumped him, blah, blah, blah." I slowly return to my full standing position, making sure my blood flow gradually returns to my head, before catching up to the "energizer bunny," who is now, by the way, walking backwards while chatting with me. *Really? Can't stand still for even a few minutes?*

G.L. Ross

"Miss Lisa, you do have the worst luck when it comes to men." *Well aren't you preaching to the choir?*

"When the time is right, my prince will ride in and sweep me off my feet." Twirling through the park I plead, "Now, please tell me we have almost hit three miles."

Turbulent Passion

Chapter Four

Sweet & Kind

Today is the day, the day I finally meet my green-eyed Goddess. After *lots* of research and trip trading, I am flying a trip with Miss Lisa Price, aka "green-eyed Goddess." I get to fly all day with her, along with a twenty hour overnight in beautiful San Diego. Miss Price is mine, all mine… after twenty long years…tonight.

Boarding the plane I feel confidant and in control, that is until I see her bent over in her black dress and boots. *Shit, I'm a goner.* The fabric enticingly clings to every beautifully sculpted curve of her body. My hands itch to cup her ass and my mouth waters at the thought of sinking my teeth into her ripe, apple shaped, butt cheek. My FO's bag ramming my ass, pulls me from my about to be bulging boner, but as I am knocked forward I find my face within kissing distance of Miss Price's delectable "apples." I quickly retrieve my balance and composure. Turning to face my First Officer, I mouth, "You are a prick."

G.L. Ross

I enter the cockpit and stow my luggage, before Lisa has a chance to turn around. Matt, the "prick," immediately steps in between us and turns on the charm, after catching a glimpse of Lisa's fine backside.

"Hey gorgeous, I am Matt, your FO. I am here to serve you with many good landings." *Really?* All I can do is stare at him as I shove my finger down my throat gagging.

Lisa is a class act and chooses to ignore his asinine statement. "Hello Matt, it is nice to meet you. Will you be taking us all the way to San Diego?" Her voice lures me. It is as sexy and smooth as melted chocolate would be dripping on her ivory, satin skin.

"Yes mam, unless you want to take a detour to Vegas to marry me?" *Okay he needs to be placed on my "no fly list" immediately.* This guy gives pilots a bad name. He has no finesse, no style. *How many days am I stuck with this jackass?*

"Sorry Matt, Vegas isn't my style. Would you like coffee or water this morning?" She is silky

Turbulent Passion

smooth, just brushed that bastard away with a smile. *I'm in love.*

"I'll take two bottles of water," Matt dejectedly answers. He tosses the bottles in his seat and informs me, without making eye contact, that he is going downstairs to do his walk around.

I proceed to pull out my paperwork and begin charting todays' flights. I'm busy at work when I hear the sexy Goddess address me, "Sir, good morning, I am Lisa. I will be flying up front today. Would you care for water or coffee this morning?" *Damn, her voice even makes me hard.*

I inhale a deep breath before turning to finally lock my blue eyes with the emerald beauties from my dreams. Miss Price shockingly gasps and tenses as our eyes meet. She looks stunned and a bit frightened. I attempt to calm her by flashing my nicest, sweetest smile.

I kindly utter my request, "I will take a coffee with one cream, Lisa." Saying her name feels like velvet caressing my lips. My entire body warms as those four letters are combined and spoken.

G.L. Ross

She knocks a stack of cups on the floor and mumbles something about being new and her first time to fly up front, while preparing my coffee. I decide to be a nice guy and calm her nerves by visiting with her. I begin to climb out of my seat. As I turn and straighten Miss Price runs smack into me with a cup of freshly brewed, extremely hot coffee. "Shit! Shit that's hot. Damn it," I exclaim.

"Sir. Oh my gosh. I am so sorry," her once controlled voice trembles with fear.

Miss Price quickly grabs a handful of paper towels and begins to pat my shirt and pants, attempting to clean her mess.

"Lisa, its fine," I snap. "Let me out of here so I can go to the lav and *I* will clean up this mess." Still a complete and nervous wreck, Miss Price bends until she is eye level with my fly. She continues patting my thickening crotch attempting to clean up the spilled coffee. I finally place my hands on her shoulders forcing her to back away from my bulging erection. Just as Lisa is realizing her effect on me, Matt, the "prick," enters the forward galley. The look on his face is priceless. I have no doubt my hands on

Turbulent Passion

Lisa's shoulders and her face at my crotch presents an interesting view, to say the least.

"New hire initiation, boss?"

As Matt laughs I mutter, "Fuck off."

Poor Lisa has no idea what is happening until she sees my bulge and hears our conversation. Completely embarrassed by my growing dick and humiliated by Matt's laughing, Lisa stands to face me. The tears in her eyes unravel me. Uncomfortable with the situation I pull a typical Lance, stating, "Not exactly the way I imagined your first hand job, Lisa."

Matt roars with laughter as Lisa disappears to the back galley completely mortified. I excuse myself to the lav to clean my pants and to release and relieve my uncomfortable manhood. Staring at my reflection in the mirror I belittle myself, "You idiot. Hand job? What a great introduction, marvelous first impression, so much for being sweet and kind. *Fuck*."

I exit the lav and am confronted by Cindy, the FA stationed in the back portion of the aircraft. "Lance, you ass, what did you say to the newbie?" Before I can even form an answer she continues,

G.L. Ross

"Not everyone thinks you are charming and will put up with your sexual bull shit. You want a harassment charge?" *Double Fuck!*

Mortified

Mortified is an understatement.

I cringe while describing my horrific scene to Haley, "Oh. My. Gosh. Haley! I am an idiot. Patting his balls? What the hell was I thinking?"

Haley grabs my shoulders, redirects my attention, and firmly explains what I need to do. *Haley is very motherly.* She knows how to tactfully be stern yet comforting at the same time. She takes charge. "First, calm down and fix your make-up. I wish I could give you a shot of whiskey, but I think you want to keep your job. Second, you need to act as though nothing happened. Brush it off and move forward. Want me to fly up front and you work the middle?"

"Thanks, but no, I have to face him eventually. I'm humiliated, completely and totally

Turbulent Passion

humiliated," I spout while pacing the galley. "Lucy warned me about him. She said to keep my distance, but what do I do? I go and play with his junk," I exclaim as my hands fist on my hips.

After repairing my make-up, I head towards the front galley where I run into Cindy. She informs me, "I set him straight and threatened him with sexual harassment charges. He will not bother you again."

"Sexual harassment? Cindy, no, I wouldn't go that far. It was my fault, not his." *WTH!*

"His 'hand job' comment was out of line." *True, but that kinda was what I was doing.* Mortified, completely mortified...

"Okay. Thanks?" I sheepishly respond. Is this day almost over?

I return to the front entry as the passengers begin to board. I notice Lance is in his seat with his back to me. I continue welcoming passengers, make my announcements, and complete my paperwork. As we begin to push from the gate I enter the cockpit and hand him the final count, "148, sir."

G.L. Ross

Off handedly he remarks, "Thank you," without looking my way. Our fingers brush as we pass the piece of paper between us; electricity sparks and crackles causing the hairs on my arms to rise. My body heat inches higher and higher. Lance's eyes abruptly dart to mine. After a few seconds he mouths, "Sorry about before." His eyes scorch my skin. My heart leaps into my throat, my pulse races, and for the first time in my life I understand how it feels to know a man's touch without physically being stroked. Our eyes continue to communicate while I slowly close the cockpit door. Captain Lance Miller may be a dangerous wolf, but at this very moment I wish the wolf would devour me.

Turbulent Passion

Chapter Five

Gentleman

As soon as we check into the hotel Lisa and the other FA's head upstairs to change their clothes, for walking and shopping in beautiful San Diego.

I decide to hit the work-out room. I desperately need to burn off this pent up energy the Goddess has built and stirred in me. I stayed professional and kept my distance the rest of the day, even though it absolutely tortured every fiber of my body, but now I want her - by my side, in my bed, under me, over me, any way imaginable - more than ever.

I stop by the front desk to cash a check, after completing my strenuous work-out. Upon hearing their laughter, I turn and glimpse the Texas trio. My eyes are immediately drawn and glued to the Goddesses' tight, curvy ass in bright yellow short nylon shorts. *And I do mean short!* The energy I just burned off is now being replaced by lethal doses of testosterone. It seems every time I see her she is more gorgeous, sexier. *How is that possible?*

G.L. Ross

"So ladies, where are you headed?" I inquire. The ladies stop and turn towards my smooth, deep voice. Walking towards them I continue, "No doubt to break some sailor's heart." I tower a full foot over my petite Goddess. Looking down towards her white tank top my eyes can't help but linger over her voluptuous cleavage. *To be so petite she is definitely blessed up top.* I ache to touch her flesh. I desperately want my tongue on her hard, erect, perky nipples. *Is she excited to see me or just cold from the air conditioner?*

Cindy redirects my eyes with her stern, clipped voice, "We completed a brisk walk, and now we are going shopping at the mall, then heading back here for dinner on the terrace." *I think Cindy needs to get laid and soon.*

"Perhaps I will join you ladies for dinner." Lisa's eyes briefly flash with excitement or perhaps I imagined the spark. "My treat, it is the least I can do after our tumultuous start today." I catch an apprehensive glance from Lisa as her cheeks transition to a petal pink flush.

Turbulent Passion

Cindy expeditiously begins declining my invitation, but Lisa smiles and intercedes, "That would be very nice, Lance." Her smile releases fireworks trapped inside me. The sound of her sultry, alto voice saying my name ignites a fire within my core. *What is it about this girl?*

I dig deep, gather my "cool" composure, and respond, "Then ladies have fun. I will see you on the terrace at 6:30. Try not to mangle too many young hearts." I present a wry smile and saunter off to my room. *Act cool Lance...act cool.*

I reach my room and immediately jump into a cold shower. *Acting cool was just that...acting.* It doesn't take long for me to realize nothing and no one will ever erase the Goddess from my mind. Conceding defeat, I turn on the hot water, grab the soap and imagine my green-eyed Goddess as I relieve my *blue* balls.

****

Six thirty couldn't get here fast enough. "A cold shower, a hot shower, a release, along with khaki cargo shorts, a pressed white linen shirt, and

G.L. Ross

cologne – check. I am ready." Upon entering the terrace I am greeted by the trios' laughter. "Hello ladies, was the shopping trip successful?" *Oh my Lord. Skin!* Bare, beautiful shoulders, lightly kissed by the sun. She is trying to kill me. *This woman will be the death of me.*

I try to breathe and not drool while Haley gives me a synopsis of the day's activities. "Lisa bought out the place, but Cindy and I enjoyed her fashion show of potential outfits."

"I see. So is this one of your acquisitions?" I inquire with a genuine smile and a naughty spark in my eyes. *Who can't smile when in the presence of this ray of sunshine?* Her energy is contagious. She exudes kindness and sweetness. She glows from within and her sun kissed shoulders gleam against her purple and green strapless sundress. She is one of a kind. *She's a Goddess-My gorgeous Goddess.*

Before Lisa is able to respond Haley interjects, "Yes it is and it is my favorite."

"Lisa, please stand and model," I request. My eyes soak in her radiant skin as her cheeks blush.

Turbulent Passion

Lisa protest, "No, come on let's order. The waiter is here, waiting on us to make a decision."

I address the young waiter, "Sir, wouldn't you like to see Miss Price model her new outfit?" The waiter also blushes as he nods his head in agreement. "Lisa, put the guy out of his misery. Stand and model," I encourage.

Embarrassed, Lisa stands to display her delicious figure and nice dress. *She could wear burlap and look incredible.* Twirling my finger I motion her to spin for the full effect, of her womanly mountains and valleys, *along with the outfit.* With her eyes locked on mine, she twirls while flashing her stunning smile. Her long blond hair lifts from her bare shoulders and beautiful back. I feel as though I am watching a perfume commercial in slow motion. Realizing I am gaping I turn and chat with the waiter, "Worth the nod, huh?" I decide it's time to redirect the kids' attention and request a bottle of chardonnay for the table.

"Lisa, thank you for the show. I am not sure who blushed more, you or the waiter?" Pulling out her chair, *yes I can be a gentleman when I try*, I

notice the ladies relaxing and laughing. I think I may
have made amends.

Seductress

"Arguing with yourself is useless," I
exasperatedly wail at the dimly lit bathroom mirror.
"Why is he so mind numbingly hot?" The entire time
I sat across from him at dinner I imagined how his
full, sensual lips would feel on mine. The scorching
heat from his eyes melted away my clothing, *at least
in my mind*. I know he undressed me with his steamy,
sky blue eyes. I could feel his strong, protective
hands wrapping around and caressing my slender
waist. I imagined the feel of his long fingers inside
me. *What the hell, Lisa? But, did you see his
glistening muscles after his work out? Damn, the man
is fine.*

I scream with frustration, "He is a player.
Lucy warned me. I have to erase him from my
thoughts!"

Twenty minutes later, after fifty sit-ups and
twenty-five push-ups, I climb into bed to read my

Turbulent Passion

Joyce Meyer book. *Clean up your thoughts, Lisa. Focus on the lesson,* from Joyce.

Thirty minutes later I realize I have re-read the same three sentences fifteen times. *Crap!* "Why does this gorgeous, enticing…*manwhore* control my thoughts? Is this why all the women throw themselves at him?" *Just give up and go to sleep and by all means stop talking out loud to yourself!* Tomorrow will be a new day, without Captain Lance Miller.

I turn off the light and grab my king size feather pillow. Hugging the pillow my thoughts begin to haze. I fade into a twilight state imagining all of us back at the Italian themed terrace. The ladies are laughing and telling stories about their various overnights in the "good old days," the days prior to September 11th. Haley and Cindy are sharing wild beach bash stories when I catch Lance's sizzling stare directed towards me. His saucy sizzle entices and arouses me. He lifts a corner of his mouth into a salacious smirk when he realizes he's been caught. My heart and pulse begin to race. I remove my foot from my soft gold, woven, platform sandal and slide

G.L. Ross

my bare, slender foot up his muscular calf. At first he jumps, slightly startled, but then he curiously scans the table to see who is playing "footsie," never imagining it will be me, he looks to me last. I flash him a mischievous grin as I pretend to pay attention to the ladies' stories. He seems interested and intrigued, so I slide my foot further, up the inside of his thigh, catching a toe on the inside of his cargo shorts. Lance grabs his ice cold draft beer, downs it, and motions to the waiter for another. Cindy lifts the empty wine bottle motioning to our waiter for another, also. *It seems we are a thirsty bunch or perhaps we are all replacing sex with alcohol.*

Lance edges his chair forward and wraps his large, warm hands around my foot. Now it is my turn to grab an alcoholic beverage. I empty my glass of wine and motion the waiter to refill my glass, from the new bottle he is holding. I'm a lightweight when it comes to drinking. Three glasses of wine and I am feeling no pain, no pain at all. Lance massages my instep with his skilled fingers and I swear I have an orgasm as my head drops backwards. If those magic fingers can do *that* massaging my foot then *please, oh please* come massage the rest of me.

Turbulent Passion

He releases my foot, in order to remove his wallet from his back pocket. *Oh no, please hurry back.* The waiter hands him the bill to visually check, before leaving with Lance's Platinum American Express card. I seize the opportunity and place my warm foot between his legs. *Thank goodness for tablecloths.* My toes inch forward to find his already growing bulge pressing against his zipper. His eyes fly open wide and lock on mine. The intensity of his stare stimulates my wild desire to be beneath him. I calmly, *or somewhat calmly,* sip my wine and massage his manhood with my adept toes. *The manwhore is having a very difficult time maintaining his composure.* It is quite interesting to "turn the table" and see Lance lose control. He readjusts himself in the chair as I feel his dick hardening and lengthening beneath my toes. He reaches for a napkin to pat the increasing perspiration glistening on his gorgeous face and then downs another cold beer.

I laughingly inquire, "Anyone else hot in here?" Cindy and Haley are so enthralled in their own conversation and bottle of wine they don't even realize I am speaking. I push my heel down and forward against his engorged balls, while my toes

G.L. Ross

continue to stimulate his erect, thickening rod. Once Lance drops his head back with a moan, I remove my foot and finish my glass of chilled wine.

I grab my clutch purse and stand to leave. "Ladies, I think it is time for me to 'hit the hay,' anyone else ready to head upstairs?" Lance exhibits shock and frustration, before blushing when I direct my attention towards him. *I made him blush!* There is absolutely no way he can stand to leave, without total embarrassment. He is trapped. *I have trapped the International Air playboy.*

Cindy and Haley empty their glasses nodding they are also ready to leave. Haley tipsily pops the question, "You ready Lance?" I can't help but giggle as I lift an inquiring eyebrow in his direction.

Lance cuts his eyes my way, before returning his attention to Haley. "You ladies head on up. I am going to have one more beer. It has been an incredible evening." When he mentions "incredible" he hungrily gazes my direction. His crystal blue eyes have darkened to a powerful navy blue tint, due to the inescapable sexual energy expanding between us.

Turbulent Passion

Haley and Cindy thank Lance, grab their purses, and direct their steps towards the lobby. While circling the table I seductively engage Lance's attention, before leaning in to hug him. *Yes, I am aware it was wicked of me to tantalize him, but it was sooo much fun.* I lean forward intentionally brushing my breast against his chin. With my lips against his ear I breathlessly whisper, "No need to stand Lance. Thanks for the memorable evening." He roughly jerks my breast to his mouth, his tongue actively searches for my erect nipple...*What the hell?*

I shoot straight up in the hotel bed wide awake from my soaking wet dream *and I don't mean sweat wet!* I have to forget this man! "Lance Miller get the hell out of my head and my bed," I shriek.

G.L. Ross

Turbulent Passion

Chapter Six

Playboy

Today I am enjoying the company of three very good looking Chicago flight attendants on our way to an overnight in sunny, Hollywood, California. I need a distraction from the onslaught of feelings I'm experiencing for Lisa and now I have three very lovely ones.

I'm so damn confused and baffled by the effect Lisa has on me. Women have always thrilled me. I love the way they smell and feel. Their hair, lingerie, giggles and smiles entice and excite me. God truly exceeded all expectations when he created the female form. There is nothing more sensational than a woman's curves. All afternoon I imagined the Goddesses' curves, especially her plentiful cleavage. *Thank God for autopilot.*

I'm relieved the work day is complete and now it is time for my Chicago "triple play." As usual, on longer overnights, the entire crew is downstairs at the hotel bar for "crew debrief." A cute, curvy blond, with *hazel* eyes keeps attempting to capture my attention. Now normally I would be all over her,

G.L. Ross

wanting to tap that new, young piece, but every time I look at her I see Lisa's emerald green eyes, her breathtaking smile, and I hear her lascivious voice. *This obsession has to stop. I am not a one woman man. I'm not!*

"Another round over here," I shout to the waitress, "on my tab." The "piece" is stroking my thigh under the table. Her strokes continue to move their way inward and upward. Maybe after a couple more drinks I will forget her eyes aren't green.

Several drinks later the "piece" and I end up in my hotel room with her naked in the center of my bed. The entire time I'm sucking on her oversized man made tit the green-eyed Goddess continues to pop into my mind. I find myself comparing the "piece" to the Goddess. The young piece's breasts aren't real like the Goddesses and the ass I'm grabbing and squeezing isn't ripe, apple round, and tight. With all of these female anatomical comparisons spinning in my head my other head keeps going up and down, up and down. *Damn it! Get out of my mind, Goddess.* The enormity of my desire to bury myself in Lisa's satiny slickness is slowly and painfully ruining my life.

With her legs spread wide the piece lifts her head to inquire, "Hey gorgeous, what's going on?"

"Nothing, don't talk. Put this on me," I order after ripping the package open with my teeth. Imagining my green-eyed Goddess beneath me my erection becomes wide and long. I hear Goddesses substitute gasp as she unrolls the condom over my girth. *Yea baby, it's all me. The rumors are actually true.* I forcefully grab and lift her hips plunging deeply into her while imagining my Goddess. I ride her roughly, but she doesn't seem to mind. I'll take care of her and make sure she cums, after I forget those *damn* green eyes.

Student

"This thesis may kill me," I scream while throwing my papers in the air. Beyond frustrated, I rack my brain for anyone who might be able to help me… *Stephen.* Maybe Stephen will have some advice. I'll give him a call.

G.L. Ross

Stephen is definitely the one that got away, handsome in a clean cut almost nerdy way, which attracts me now, but didn't three to five years ago. In my early twenties I wanted the smooth talking, dark hair, mesmerizing eyes of a bad boy and boy did I go through them. They all cheated on me; if you call cheating dating others behind my back, always because I wouldn't have sex with them. But Stephen was always there to hear me moan and groan about them. *I guess I owe him a counseling fee.*

"Stephen. Hey it's Lisa, how are you?"

"Oh my goodness, it is great to hear from you. You still as gorgeous as ever?" *I love this man.*

"Stephen, why didn't I marry you?" I am smiling ear to ear. I really do love this man.

"Lisa, you wouldn't even go on a date with me; most of my friends, yes; me, no." I can hear the pain behind the teasing, in his voice. I know I hurt him, which in turn hurts me.

"I was an idiot back then." I flop onto my bed, staring at the popcorn ceiling.

Turbulent Passion

"It wasn't that long ago, silly."

"Long enough. So how is Terri?" Terri is the brilliant woman who married this prince of a man.

"She is fine. She puts up with me. Did you know we are expecting?"

"What?" I sit up and lean back against the headboard. "A baby?"

"Yes, what else could it be?" Stephen laughs. *I love his laugh.*

"I don't know a car or a dog, maybe. You are so young." I really want his life; a spouse, expecting a child, a real home. I know I am not supposed to lust for someone else's life, but I really screwed up not dating Stephen.

"Well, we're excited and feel very blessed." *Earth to Lisa...*

"Of course, I'm so sorry for my reaction. I really am happy for you, congratulations. You will be an incredible father. I know Terri thanks God every

G.L. Ross

day for bringing you into her life. I would. I do. You are a true friend."

"Lisa, why so sentimental?" Stephen always could read me well.

"Just watching the time flying by me and wondering if I will ever find 'Mr. Right.' My friends all seem to settle with 'Mr. Right Now,' but I don't want that." *Hear I go again crying and whining to Stephen.*

"No, you shouldn't. Do not settle, Lisa. God will send you 'Mr. Right' at the appointed time, be patient and wait. Now that we have straightened that out, why did you really call?"

As I mentioned, he reads me well. "I need help with my thesis, Mr. PhD."

****

Finally, thesis finished and submitted. I had to request a two week extension, but it was well worth it, at least in my opinion. I hope the professor agrees. Stephen's suggestions helped, but required extra research, which meant extra time. Anyway, it's

Turbulent Passion

done and is no longer devouring my life and apartment.

Speaking of my apartment it might as well have a revolving door. Seems all I ever do is empty my suitcase, wash clothes, and put them back in the suitcase to fly again. I spent my entire vacation week finishing my thesis - *some vacation*. So, I've decided I deserve a mini-vacation, a weekend get-away. I reside in the largest state in the USA- Texas, *or is it California?* Anyway, it is big and I have never even been everywhere the great lone star state has to offer. So, I am heading south to Galveston. I love the beach! The car, the road, and my thoughts equal a road trip.

Saturday morning and my flight's wide open, *thank goodness*. Since I have to be at work on Tuesday, I decided it would make more sense to fly to Houston, rent a car with my great discount, and drive to Galveston. I was able to get a reservation for Saturday and Sunday night at my favorite hotel, which is on the beach. Most of the Galveston hotels are across the road from the beach, because of the

G.L. Ross

seawall, but I have a favorite that is a few miles down the road near seashell filled Jamaica beach.

"Hey Jim, how is it going? Why are you here working an am shift?" Jim is one of my favorite Operations Agents in the Dallas/Fort Worth airport. He gives the flight attendants time to run off and get food, before boarding the flights. Sometimes he even delivers iced teas and lattes to us as a special treat. Plus, he is sweet and always has a bright, beaming smile, most likely because all the flight attendants flirt with him.

"Overtime, extra money, I need money to afford to take you flight attendants out. Where are you headed, Lisa?"

"The beach, for the weekend. Sun, fun, and alcoholic beverages," I answer with a twinkle in my eyes.

"Well, have fun. Call me if I need to come bail you out of jail."

"Good one Jim. Appreciate ya." I hug my dear friend and head down the jetway to board my

Turbulent Passion

flight, off to the stress free beach and a *"Lance free zone."*

"Welcome to Houston Hobby Airport," the flight attendant announces upon arrival. While deplaning I participate in my off the wall activity of talking to myself, "Now I'll get the car and off to the beach." Out of nowhere a guy runs into me and almost knocks me to the ground. "Ouch. Look where you are going. You just tripped me," I reprimand.

"Sorry." While checking me out head to toe the ruggedly handsome man begins to stumble over an apology, "Really, I am sorry. I was looking down at my paperwork and didn't see you. My bad." *Why do I feel I am being undressed?*

I give him my patronizing smile. "Yes, it is your fault, but since you are a fellow employee I will give you a break."

"Ha. Well isn't that generous of you. What department do you work in?" He has a wicked, bad boy vibe about him and he makes me feel…weird, for lack of a better description. Plus, he's a smart ass. I need to steer clear of him.

G.L. Ross

I nonchalantly answer, "Inflight, I am a flight attendant out of Dallas/Fort Worth. You must be an OPS agent." *OPS stands for Operations Agents, the airline industry has its own lingo.*

"Correct, I'm Wayne and you are?" He extends his hand for me to shake. I notice his eyes; they are dark, taunting, almost secretive. *Maybe that is why I feel...weird.*

I shake his hand and introduce myself, "My name is Lisa, Lisa Price."

"Well, Lisa, Lisa Price, it is nice to meet you." *Smart ass.* "What brings you to Houston?" We walk over to the side of the gate area, so the other passengers may deplane.

"I'm on my way to Galveston to relax in the sun, but first I have to get my rental car. I was on my way when you ran over me." *Yes, I too can be a smart ass.*

Wayne leans an arm against the light blue carpeted wall, striking a pose. "Well, Lisa Price, I live in Clearlake which is on the way to Galveston. Do you have dinner plans tonight?" He seems nice

Turbulent Passion

enough, even though he is a cocky smart ass who makes me feel weird, but I don't really want to deal with someone. I want a "man free zone" and dinner would require applying make-up. Lucy would say to go, but I don't think so.

"Is that a difficult question?" *Oh, he is a royal smart ass.*

"Excuse me, kind of zoned out thinking of my plans." *And the fact you are a cocky, smug, SOB.* "I really was planning on taking it easy tonight."

"How about lunch tomorrow? I'll meet you at Landry's, right off the seawall, easy to find. How about 12:30?"

He is persistent. It's only lunch and I have to eat…"Well, okay, but please be casual."

"It is the only way I know to be." *Maybe I will like him after all.*

"Good. Okay. Well Wayne, since I'm meeting you for lunch perhaps I should know your last name." *I love counter-serving smart ass, especially with guys who are cocky.*

G.L. Ross

Wayne laughs. "Brighton, Wayne Brighton."

"Well, Wayne Brighton, I will see you tomorrow at 12:30." I toss my long, blond hair over my shoulder and walk like I know he is watching, because I *know* he is.

****

My favorite part, of an early morning, is a long walk on the beach. The sound of the ocean waves centers me. It seems all my worries are carried away with the tide. I guess I really am a true Pisces. The view of the waves breaking and frothing soothes all of my stress induced pains. I need to move here. I love being right here on the sand, playing in the water, *so why on earth did I agree to meet Wayne for lunch?* I would much rather be stretched out here on the sand all day. He seemed nice enough, in fact kind of funny, beneath his cockiness. *I like guys who make me laugh.* But, I came here to be alone.

It's only lunch. I will have a nice meal, be cordial, and be gone in two hours max. I really don't have a choice since I failed to get his digits. Lucy

Turbulent Passion

will be happy I'm going out. *We won't mention I'm not wearing make-up.* I am kissed by the sun, which is all the make-up required. *LOL.* It'll take me twenty minutes to drive in and park, so I can stay on the beach until 11:30. I'll take a quick shower, apply some mascara, lip gloss, and be on my way. My hair can dry while I am driving. *I'm on vacation and honestly wish I had never met Wayne Brighton.*

I arrive at Landry's at 12:20 in white shorts, a hot pink halter top, and matching pink flip flop sandals. Wayne is already here. He looks nice in his khaki shorts, blue linen shirt, sandals, and Ray-Bans; maybe this won't be so bad after all. "Hey Wayne, thanks for being casual."

"Hi Lisa, looks like you got some sun yesterday. You have a glow about you."

"Thanks." Breathe Lisa. I hate dating!

The waiter seats us at a table near the front window where we are able to enjoy the tranquilizing effect of the ocean view. *Look at the ocean, watch the waves, and relax, Lisa. Try to have fun.* Wayne and I place our order, enjoy the scrumptious fresh

G.L. Ross

seafood, and chat for an hour non-stop. Wayne is surprisingly easy to chat with, very relaxed and subdued; nothing resembling the egomaniac I met at the airport. Normally I have to carry the conversation when out with someone new, but Wayne has all kinds of stories about several of the airlines. His dad served in the Air Force, so Wayne lived all over the world. We are engrossed in a story about living in Asia when the waiter approaches our table, displaying a delicious array of desserts. "Dessert, Lisa?" Wayne offers.

"No, but thanks. I am stuffed." *I feel like a beached whale.* "Please roll me across the street to the beach." We continue laughing as the waiter drops off the check. Seeing the check on the table reminds me of Lance reaching for his wallet, in my dream. My mind suddenly overflows with sexual foot images. I feel my cheeks turning a crimson shade of red. *Clear your mind, Lisa.*

Ever the gentleman, Wayne snags and pays the bill. Exiting the restaurant he asks, "How about we go walk this off? Take a walk on the beach?" I definitely need to walk all these calories off. *Thank*

Turbulent Passion

*goodness airlines do not have weight check anymore.
I know...vague, where did that thought come from?
My mind is all over the place these days. Focus, Lisa,
on Wayne.*

"Sure, sounds like a great plan." Even if he
is a bit cocky, at least he is romantic. A walk on the
beach is subtly sexy and definitely fairy-tale-"ish."
Maybe he is the "one," which is why I felt weird
around him yesterday. *Stop analyzing and trying to
decipher everything – enjoy the attention and the
beach.*

Lunch turns into dinner and dinner into a
nightcap. Wayne captivates my attention and I
honestly think I capture a part of his heart. "Wayne, I
really need to get back to the hotel. I'm flying out at
noon tomorrow, so I need to get organized. Walk me
to my car?"

"Sure. Sorry I monopolized your time," he
says with a half grin.

"Wayne you didn't monopolize my time.
I've had fun." I smile at him, with my timid, shy

G.L. Ross

look, the look where I gaze through my lashes. *It always gets to men.*

"Lisa, you are one terrific lady." He laces his fingers with mine as we cross the street and head to my rental car.

Nervous energy lingers in the air, so I launch into a conversation, "How long have you lived in Houston?"

"Five years but that is soon to change. I put in a transfer and it was approved, so I'm moving to Austin in two weeks." *I love Austin.*

"Austin is a great town. I love my overnights there, especially 6th Street. Maybe I'll see you on an Austin overnight." I attempt to release Wayne's hand, in order to dig the keys out of my purse. Instead he pulls me towards him, so we are face to face beside the car. *My heart is pounding through my chest.*

Wayne's voice oozes a passionate lilt, "Lisa that is a date I am holding you to, so when is your next Austin overnight?" He leans and embraces my face in his large hands. Our eyes engage as he lightly

Turbulent Passion

slides his knuckle down my cheek. My stomach flutters when he gently presses his lips to mine. He is tender and supercalifragilisticexpialidocious sexy. *It seemed the only appropriately descriptive word.*

A tingling sensation spreads through my limbs. Wayne traces my lips with his tongue before brushing his lips across mine once more. I've never been kissed like this. My pulse races up and down my body. Lost in the seductively sensual moment I slowly open my eyes before whispering my reply, "In two weeks."

G.L. Ross

Turbulent Passion

Chapter Seven

Sweets

I am losing it. It's been three, long, agonizing weeks since I spent time with Lisa. I passed her in the airport a week ago, but it was so brief it doesn't even count. She didn't see me, but I saw her flirting with Jim. I realize Jim flirts with all the girls, but the thought of someone else being the recipient of her smile, of her attention, of her hugs, well it drives me fuckin'nuts.

The past three weeks I have had more cold showers and long work-out sessions then I have had since my early twenties. I went on a date, *yea, a real date not a "fuck and go,"* but for the first time I can ever remember I took my date home after dinner. She was gorgeous *and built*, but I couldn't even concentrate on her cleavage or her extremely long, limber legs. So, I, Lance Miller, have remained abstinent for two weeks. *Two fucking, miserable weeks.* This chick has me acting like a teenage boy with a tube of lube.

Damn it! I swore a woman would never control me or my thoughts, but I can't get this one

G.L. Ross

out of my head. *Goddess has to go or else belong to me and only me.*

****

The Cancun hotel has a terrific bar and a ton of crews overnight at this hotel, so Cancun is always a party waiting to happen. John, my FO, and I have arranged three rectangular tables to seat four or five crews. I've chosen a seat where I can inspect the sweet treats checking in the hotel. *Working for International is the grown-up version of enjoying a candy store, so many sweet, scrumptious treats waiting to be licked and enjoyed.* The confectionary temptations must be displayed for John and me in order to enter the elevator. This way I am able to extend my own, personal invitation for the crews to join us. *The ladies treasure the personal attention, especially since I am the whip cream and cherry topping their sugary delights.*

Several hours after our arrival the bar is abuzz with energy, laughter, and conversation. Four beers and two shots later I excuse myself to take a leak. I thought she might be here tonight, *the Goddess*, but I guess it was wishful thinking.

Turbulent Passion

I refresh my face with a splash of cold water and catch a glimpse of my reflection in the mirror. *Who am I?* I don't recognize the man staring back. *What has happened to me?* I'm almost thirty four years old and have never had a serious relationship. Sure, I've had my share of females, but nothing remotely serious and steady. Even in high school I kept the girls rotating. They knew if they didn't put out I was moving on so they gave me what I wanted whether it be a blow job or spread eagle in the back of my pick-up truck. I was the quarterback everyone wanted on their arm, so with demand I received my supply. *I sound like an asshole.*

Why am I like this? What caused me to have such little respect for women?

Maybe I just have a *lot* of respect for myself. That's it. I like women, but I come first. *I have to make myself first, because life has proven no one else will.*

Heading back to the table I contemplate which of the gals in the bar I should bang tonight. "Hey John, any new crews arrive?" I graze my hand across the nipples of blond #1 while climbing over

G.L. Ross

her chair to my seat. She smiles and gives me a wink. *Maybe I'll bang her.*

"Yea, a Dallas/Fort Worth crew arrived. Paul Johnson and Mike somebody. They are coming downstairs with their flight attendants."

Not caring that blond #1 or #2 can hear me I inquire, "Any of the gals hot?"

With a huge smile John replies, "Uh yea. Two are lookers and one of them is built. I mean built like a brick house."

"Blond or brunette?" I ask.

"Blond."

"Then she is mine."

"Hey man, I saw her first," John complains.

"I am pulling rank. She is mine, unless of course I have already tasted her delicious treats. If I have appreciated her fine cuisine then she is yours." The cute waitress arrives with the shots of tequila I ordered, prior to going to the loo. John and I down our shots; I stretch, grab blond #2, pull her onto my

Turbulent Passion

lap, and suck my slice of lime. *Life is good.* As I stare into the valley of blond #2's mountainous cleavage I decide she may be a keeper for tonight. *Let me check her ass.* I rub my hand across her plump curvature and decide she is worth spending money on to get drunk.

"Hey sweetie," I yell. The young, wide-eyed waitress lights up as she acknowledges my presence. *They all do that. Got to love it!* "Bring us another round, doll, on my tab." I flash my, "I know you want me," smile as she nods okay and turns five shades of red. Having that effect on women, of any age, never gets old.

"Hey Lance, that's the blond," John states.

"Where?" I stand to search the room, but I don't see a blond I haven't already checked out. About two seconds later, I feel an arm wrapping tightly around my neck. "Who the hell has me?" I gruffly reply.

"Lance, how the hell are you?"

"I would know that voice anywhere," I retort. Standing behind me I find my Air Force buddy

G.L. Ross

Mike Ford. "How are you, man? I haven't seen you in almost two years." Mike's still trim and athletically built. *He never was a muscular, beefy guy.* He's still sporting the crew cut we all wore in the Air Force, and he wears it well. Many women are really enjoying the view of Mike's physique, in his jeans and white, tight fitting t-shirt. *Go Air Force!*

"I've been out in Atlanta. I recently changed my base to DFW. You a Captain in Big D?"

"Hell yea, maybe we can fly together soon. You a right seater?"

"Yea, but not for long. I can upgrade to Captain in about a year. So Lance, you still a hound dog or has someone tied you down?" I flash him my middle finger, before showing my bare ring finger.

"Trust me they have tied me down, but with silk ties and ropes."

I flash a cocky smile before grabbing blond #2 by her ass and placing her back on my thigh, *strategically keeping my hand under her.*

Turbulent Passion

"Damn. Some things never change." That's right, keep admiring the master.

"How about you? Married? Kids?" I ask, while copping a feel of the abundant ass in my left hand.

"No, not yet, but if I have my way I'm marrying a flight attendant I met today. She's on my crew." Mike's scanning the crowd for his future bride.

"Oh really? Where is she? Have I 'had' her?" This time Mike flashes me his middle finger.

"Really Lance? You are crass. I can guarantee you haven't 'had' this one." Mike stops his search and refocuses his attention on me. "She is sweet, pure, and about to be all mine. She came downstairs with me." Mike searches the room again as he continues, "Paul grabbed us a table across from the end of this table. You need to come meet her."

"You think you can trust me with her?" My eyes freeze at her icy stare.

G.L. Ross

I hear Pauls' booming voice shouting a drink order from across the room. "Mike, grab two merlots, one chardonnay, a scotch and water, and whatever you want."

My face falls as the Goddess and I stare intensely at each other. I push blond #2 from my lap landing her splat on the floor. In my zombie-like stance, I stand frozen, staring at Lisa.

"Lance Miller, how the hell are you?" Paul has made his way across the room to shake my hand. Blond #2 returns to her feet and shoots me a go to hell look as she chooses to relocate to the end of the table. Over Paul's shoulder, I see the Goddess lower her repulsed eyes and turn her back to me. *Life has become way too complicated, in such a short period of time.*

Paul and I converse for about fifteen minutes. I convince him we need to move our reunion to his table. I have to straighten everything out with Lisa. I have no clue how to explain my actions, except I'm an asshole. But, in my defense, I wouldn't treat her that way. She has to believe me. Why should she believe me? I am fucked up!

Turbulent Passion

Paul's crew is seated at a round cherry table, except for Lisa who is presently MIA. Paul and I reach the table simultaneously with Lisa, as she returns from the ladies' room. Mike leaps to his feet to pull out Lisa's chair. She flashes him an approving, adoring smile. He is turning on the charm and my blood is boiling. If she wants "old fashioned" manners, courting manners, I can do that. *I've never done it before, but I can search on Google and learn.* Never have I wanted to obliterate one of my buddies, especially over a girl, but she is *my* Goddess and I'll be damned if he gets this girl.

Sparks

Janet's pulling off her black leather boots in the hotel lobby as Andrea signs us into the hotel. "My feet are kill-ing me. I haven't been this happy to see a hotel in years. I hear a hot bath and a chilled glass of wine calling my name."

"But, you are coming downstairs to join us for a glass of wine, prior to the tub, right?" I pretend to pout until Janet reluctantly agrees to join us.

G.L. Ross

"Okay one glass, but that is it." She says that now, but once she joins us she will stay for two or three glasses.

Andrea is sorting our keys and figuring out our lobby time when I hear a burst of laughter followed by a voice I recognize. I tense and softly mutter to myself, "Please don't let it be him. Please don't let it be him." I peek around the corner and low and behold Captain Lance Miller is holding court. He's surrounded by busty, blond, long legged females. One is rubbing his shoulders; another is shoving her cleavage in his face, while one more entices him by stroking his firm, muscular thigh. *Do these gals have no shame?*

"Lisa, who are you watching?" Andrea's standing behind me peering over my shoulder. "Here's your key," she absently responds while searching, for the object of my attention. When her gaze settles upon Lance her eyes light up and a huge smile crosses her face. *Not her too.* "No wonder your face is red. He is a gorgeous specimen of manhood and that laugh makes me tingle in special areas." *Andrea!* "Come on let's change clothes and join the

Turbulent Passion

fun." *Somehow watching Lance and the blond bimbo's does-not-sound-fun.*

Due to dreading the walk past him, I decide to postpone the inevitable, and choose to cash a check at the front desk. "I need to get some cash. You guys go on. You don't have to wait for me." *Please, please go on and I will sneak upstairs. I promise to never answer my phone or a knock on my door until lobby time tomorrow. Please God.*

Janet interjects, "No hurry, we will wait." *Damn it, damn it, damn it!*

She continues, "I have to find the strength or numbness, in my feet, to be able to walk again." While Janet tries to rub feeling back into her feet I slowly write my check. He needs to look away so I can get by him without creating a scene. *I can't believe the way those hussies hang on him.*

"You still drinking him in?"

"What?" Andrea has caught me again. "No just staring into space while the clerk gets my cash."

G.L. Ross

"Right…sure Lisa. Remember there's no crime in 'reading the menu.' I would absolutely love to taste and lick him."

"Andrea!" Andrea is licking her lips while I'm attempting to retrieve my jaw from the floor. *He has the same damn effect on every breathing female form.* I need to forget Lance and remember my rule regarding pilots. *Pilots + Lisa + Dating = Not Happening!*

Andrea pulls Janet up from the couch while I thank the clerk who has returned with my cash. We all grab our roller bags and make our way past the viewing runway. Not wanting to make eye contact as I walk past him I avert my eyes, until someone screams my name. *Crap!*

I yell to my friend, over the roar of conversation and music that I will be down in a second. I turn to where Lance is sitting, but he is gone. *Thank goodness. Thank you Lord Jesus.* I feel a burst of relief *mixed with regret*. Why? Why do I care? He is a player, not a keeper. He is not a "happily ever after" kind of guy, which is what I want *and deserve*, someday.

Turbulent Passion

The elevator stops at our floor before I realize I even entered an elevator. *He is making me crazy.*

"Can you ladies be ready in ten minutes?" Janet asks.

"Sure," I agree.

Andrea request fifteen minutes, before we meet in the hallway to head downstairs, so we all agree on fifteen. I toss my bag on the luggage rack, lose my balance, and fall against the king size bed. *It's simply not my night.*

Hotel rooms become my home away from home, just as the beds become my bed and the thermostat becomes my thermostat. Flight crews live odd, but interesting lives, and little things make us very happy, such as firm pillows and a super cold room. I wish I could climb into my bed right now. Maybe I should call it a night. No one would really care – would they?

I decide to stay seated on the floor as I begin to tug on my boots. I need to go downstairs with my crew. *Life can only go up from here. Ha! I have to*

G.L. Ross

laugh at the irony or else I will cry. After removing my boots, I unzip my roller bag and hang my uniform for the next day. Fortunately, I packed a cute outfit to wear tonight. I often pack only my work out clothes, but this time I packed a pair of lime green capris, with an off the shoulder hot pink and lime green ruffle top. I guarantee if Lance is down there he won't miss me in my vibrant attire.

"But, again, why do I care?" I angrily grunt to myself. Get dressed and concentrate on getting to know Mike, he seems like a nice guy, plus I'm in Austin soon which equals Wayne and dancing. Lance Miller is not on my radar, not now, not ever.

The three of us turn the corner to enter the bar and run into Mike. "Ladies, I have a table for us near the TV's. Paul is over there. See him?" Mike points towards the wide screen televisions as his other hand touches the small of my back. *There is something sensual about a man touching the small of a ladies' back. I like it.* I acknowledge seeing Paul and head his direction. Janet and Andrea stop to admire Lance. I choose to sneak behind them, away from Captain America's view.

Turbulent Passion

"Hey Paul, have your ordered?" Mike pulls out my chair as I take a menu from Paul. "Thanks guys. A girl could get used to this kind of treatment." Paul smiles and buries his head in the menu. *I guess that means he hasn't ordered.*

Mike leans next to my ear and whispers, "Then get used to it." I feel a shiver as his hands touch my shoulders. "I will be right back. I see someone I know." *Breathe Lisa.*

"Lisa, you disappeared," Janet states as she flops into her chair, grabs a menu, and removes her flip-flops to once again rub her feet. *I think she needs lower heel boots.*

"Didn't you want to see him up close?" Andrea joins in.

"There was enough drooling from you two." I look Lance's way and low and behold a blond bimbo is on his lap. Mark him off your list, Lisa. *Was he on my list?* Lucy said to steer clear of him. *Concentrate on Mark...the gentleman.*

Paul inquires, "Ladies, what's your beverage of choice for the evening?" Andrea and Janet each

G.L. Ross

order a glass of Merlot, while I choose a glass of Chardonnay. Paul proceeds to scream our beverage order, across the room, to Mike. Mike turns to acknowledge Paul when BAM, Lance and I lock eyes. My heart leaps into my throat as his face plummets. Lance swiftly stands dropping his blond bimbo to the floor. *The floor!* I don't know whether to laugh or be repulsed. I quickly divert my attention to my crew and find Paul is missing.

"Where's Paul?" I inquire.

Andrea places her menu on the table and responds, "He headed over to the beautiful male specimen."

Seriously? Does the *specimen* know everyone?

The waitress takes our food order, while Mike delivers our wine. I bat my lashes and flirtatiously respond, "Thanks, Mike" as he hands me my glass, intentionally brushing his fingers against mine. *No spark. Maybe I need to concentrate on him more, for there to be a spark.*

Turbulent Passion

We're sharing our passenger stories from the day's activities, when I excuse myself to the ladies' room. I escape into a stall to pull myself together. *Breathe Lisa.* Why am I allowing Lance to get to me? He isn't my type. He's arrogant and treats women with no respect, *but hell's bells he is gorgeous. I swear my body heats when he looks at me.* I know he is looking my way, before I even see him. *No lack of sparks when Lance is near...Crap! Crap! Crap!*

"Be strong." I exit the stall *talking to myself once again.* "Get a grip, Lisa," I spout while washing and drying my trembling hands. I blot my face with a paper towel, re-apply my lip gloss, and take a deep breath before returning to the bar. Mike stands as I enter, to once again pull my chair out for me. I may really like this southern gentleman. *Surely the sparks will ignite eventually. Right?* Janet winks at me in reference to Mike's gentlemanly actions. This is good. I'm basking in the attention when Paul and Lance pull up chairs to our table. *Quadruple crap!*

Lance winks at me and my eyes widen in disbelief. "In case you ladies haven't already met or heard of him, this is Lance Miller. Ladies introduce

G.L. Ross

yourselves," Paul instructs. *Jeez the pilots even acknowledge him with honor and worship. Whatever…*

Andrea and Janet act like blubbering, idiotic, high school teenagers introducing themselves. Lance turns for my introduction, but I change the topic to a funny incident from earlier in the day. *Score one for Lisa.* Mike pulls his chair closer to mine. Out of the corner of my eye I see Lance squeezing his chair between Andrea's and mine. *Did he not understand I'm ignoring him?* I lean in closer to try and hear what Mike is saying when I am caught off guard by the feel of Lance's hand on my thigh. First I gasp, but after a deep breath I calmly place my hand on his lifting it off my lap and back to his thigh, never removing my attention from Mike. *Two for Lisa.*

"Lisa?" I hear Lance, but pretend not to hear him. Mike turns to visit with an Atlanta co-worker and immediately I feel Lance's breath against my ear. "Lisa, you are going to have to look at me before this night is over."

"Excuse me?" I turn to face him full of inner strength and confidence, that is until I see his

Turbulent Passion

beautiful blue eyes and incredible smile. *The man is simply breathtakingly gorgeous.*

"There. See that wasn't so hard." *He is also frustratingly cocky.* I feel my blood simmering. Lance releases hostility and some other kind of raw emotion inside me. I'm never edgy or intentionally rude to people, except him.

"Hello Lance. How are you?' I exhibit calm and coolness in front of him. I remain monotone, unfeeling. *Maybe I should be an actress?*

"I am doing a lot better now, sweetheart." He slowly reaches his arm behind me to slide and rest on my chair. I have no doubt he saw me flinch, which pisses me off. *He will not win.* "Why are you ignoring me, Lisa?"

"I'm not. I am visiting with everyone. If you want someone's full attention head back over to your bimbo blonds who I am sure say, 'like' ten times in a sentence." *Did I really just say that?* Lance sits silently for about a minute and then burst into laughter. *He is laughing - at me! I want to wrap my*

G.L. Ross

hands around his throat and squeeze tightly. This man is so unbelievably frustrating.

"Have breakfast with me in the morning?" *Excuse me? What planet are you from?*

"What? You want to have breakfast with me?" This man doesn't know how to take a hint. I practically spit in his face and slapped him with my words, but he invites me to breakfast?

"You eat don't you?" He smugly asks.

Look at that arrogant, tantalizing smile. *Stay strong Lisa.* "Of course, but…"

"But nothing. What room are you in? I'll…"

"There is no way I am telling you my room number." I whip my head back to visit with Mike, but he is now sitting with the guys at the table behind us. Now I've lost the nice guy while dealing with Mr. Arrogant Ass. *Great.*

"Lisa, I simply want your number so I may meet you in the morning to walk you downstairs."

Turbulent Passion

"Oh." I sit quietly and contemplate for a few seconds before replying, "I would rather meet you in the restaurant. What time?" *Get control girl. Be the one in charge.*

"You really do not trust me. How about 9:15?" he dishearteningly responds.

It's only breakfast, Lisa. "I will be in the restaurant at 9:15. Now, please get me another glass of wine." Lance smiles and heads to the bar. I can't help but admire his fine tush perfectly hugged by his worn, faded blue jeans. *The ball is back in my court... I think.*

G.L. Ross

Turbulent Passion

Chapter Eight

Friends & Lovers

I didn't get much sleep due to a certain green-eyed Goddess, but I couldn't care less because this morning I will have her all to myself. Last night I discovered a new side to Miss Price and I must admit I desire her even more now. She didn't put up with my shit and I find that extremely hot. She didn't want me or my attention, which turns me on. But, the icing on the cake was when she implied I could never have her, well then she became a challenge. *And, I love a challenge.*

I check out my appearance in the elevator's mirrored wall. I look good. I shaved and put on cologne. My jeans fit well, *in all the right places*, and my shirt is a rad blend of purple, green, and yellow swirls, perfectly starched, and tapered to my physique. *How can she say "no" to this?*

I've made a point to be here at 9:00 sharp. I want to be waiting for Miss Price when she arrives. I wish I could order us mimosas, but we won't have

G.L. Ross

the required hours between alcohol and flying. *Hate those damn rules.*

"Good morning. May I have a table for two, in a corner if possible?"

"Certainly sir, please follow me." I follow the gentleman into the restaurant and am about to sit down when I hear her sultry, sassy tone.

"Hey handsome." I turn immediately towards her voice. "Why did I know *you* would turn to look?" *She got me there.*

"So, you're early. Eager to see me?" I ask as I recline in the seat next to her. *Of course, she chose a table in the middle of the restaurant.* So much for being intimate.

"No, I am eager to get this over with." Immediately I recognize her regret regarding her reply. "I didn't…"

Turbulent Passion

"It's fine Lisa. One of my intentions this morning is to convince you I am a nice guy." *Lightning please do not strike me dead.*

"And your other intentions?" she nervously asks.

"To become your friend and lover." Lisa spurts and chokes on her orange juice, *but this time I jump to clean her up.* "Guess I shouldn't have been quite so blunt." I seize the opportunity to pat her face *and chest* with my napkin. *Turnabout is fair play. Yes, I am grinning ear to ear.*

"Stop it Lance." She pushes my hands away while straightening her wet t-shirt, which is now clinging to her beautiful breasts and erect nipples. *Goddess has some perky, perfect tits.*

"Sorry," I say, *but do not mean.*

Thank goodness the waiter comes to take our orders so I am forced to stop staring at her amazing tits. *I'm already getting hard.* After he leaves I begin to quiz Lisa about her life, family,

G.L. Ross

activities, anything to be conversational. At first, she is hesitant to share. But, my charms wear her down. *Yes, I can be charming.* In fact, by the time we finish our meal I know: she was on the drill team, pledged a sorority, was a fraternity little sister, recently completed her master's thesis, and is even more incredible than I ever imagined. "So, what would you like to know about me?"

She sits quietly for a couple of minutes, although the minutes of silence feel like a lifetime. Finally she leans back in her chair, folds her hands in her lap, and asks, "Have you ever been in a committed relationship, Lance?"

"Well, you cut right to the chase, don't you? Am I one of your counseling patients, Lisa?

"No, but do you need to be?" She struggles to remain serious, but loses it by smiling and laughing. "You don't have to answer either question."

As Lisa reaches for her glass, I quickly reach for her hand covering it with mine. I feel an

Turbulent Passion

intense energy flowing between us. When I look at her vibrant face I see the same exact energy sparkling in her eyes. She can deny it all she wants, but she is made for me and she wants me.

I want her. Did I just admit that? Yes, I did. I really am a goner when it comes to this woman. "No Lisa, I have never been in a committed relationship; at least, not yet," I reply while holding her hand. My eyes lock on hers until she becomes uncomfortable, lowering her lashes and slowly removing her hand from mine.

It was a brief moment, but it *was* a moment.

"I have a question for you, Lance." *Finally, she wants to know about me. I am breaking through her walls.* "Do you buy your condoms in bulk to save money and are they delivered to your house monthly?"

"You really don't like me, do you?" My heart shatters, but I put on a tough guy act. I can't let her see me hurt. *What do I have to do to win her over?*

G.L. Ross

"It's not that I don't like you. I simply do not like the way you treat women."

I snap, "I treat women with the level of respect they deserve."

"Excuse me? We deserve to be treated like disposable pieces of crap that can be tossed to the floor?" *Shit, she saw that.*

Push down the anger, Lance. I attempt to cool my jets, but can't help having a tinge of anger in my tone, "Only if you are shoving your tits or ass in my face, which you will obviously never do."

Lisa's face turns blood red as she turns her body to face me head on. "You sir are a pig."

"A pig?" Damn she is cute. *Don't laugh, Lance.*

"Yes, a pig. Your problem is you simply cannot stand the fact I am immune to your 'so called' charms." Lisa stands, holding her head high, trying to appear tough. *She has her nose so high in the air she may break her neck.* She tosses her napkin on the table before finishing her retort, "Thank you for the breakfast. Fly safely."

I remain seated enjoying my coffee and the fabulous rear view of Miss Price's curvaceous body as she struts out of the restaurant, boldly swishing her hips. I can't help but laugh. She thinks she's being so mean and tough. She did everything in her power to try and piss me off so I would leave her alone, but it had an opposite effect. Rather than pushing me away, more than ever, I want to wrap my arms around her and pull her into my bed. She swept me off my feet, but now I have to figure out a way to sweep her off hers. *Man, I adore this gal.*

New & Improved

Two weeks turned into almost four. The extra days felt like a lifetime. Lucy traded trips with me, so I could finally have an Austin overnight. Wayne and I visited on the phone almost daily. Texting became an obsession. I lived for his next text. Every time the plane landed I hurried to turn on my phone. His messages would start each day with something along the line of, "Hey sunshine. Have a

G.L. Ross

great day. My day is already great because I thought of you." *Melt my heart!* What woman wouldn't adore a man who begins her day in such a special way? I have no doubt Lance would never send me such a sweet text. *Stop it, Lisa. No. More. Lance.*

Some of our texting became quite steamy, but it's a lot easier to say things via texting. I probably shouldn't have been so forward, but oh well, what is sent, is sent. Now the decision is what to wear for our date. Wayne said we would head to 6th street for dinner at a Mexican restaurant, then music at a jazz bar, followed by dancing at his favorite country western hangout.

I'm a huge country music fan. All I can think about is dancing, with Wayne's arms wrapped snugly around me, to Chris Young's, "Gettin' You Home Tonight." *Calm your heart rate, Lisa, and decide what you are wearing.*

I need something sexy, but not too sexy. I'm not planning on having sex with him, even though he is tempting. I want him to respect me. I'll wear a silk blouse, men love the feel of sex, *jeez Lisa* get your

Turbulent Passion

mind out of the gutter; they love the feel of silk! *Freudian slip?*

I relish the idea of his hand caressing the silk fabric of my blouse up and down my back. The thought brings a smile to my lips. *Anyway, back to wardrobe.* So, bottom half... maybe white jeans with nude high heeled sandals? Sexy, but understated; plus, jeans aren't easy to remove. *Yes, I have a one track mind.*

I'll wear my purple satin bra and white lace panties, or maybe I'll go commando, no need for panty lines. *What I need is a really cold shower.* Only eight more hours until I kiss Wayne and forget Lance Miller.

Thank goodness all the flights were full. The passengers kept me busy with their numerous demands so the hours flew by. Every time I turned on my phone Wayne was texting a countdown:

"Six hours until I see you."

"Five hours until I wrap my arms around you."

G.L. Ross

"Four hours until I kiss you."

"Three hours until, well still kissing you - hurry."

"Two hours until I sweep you into my arms on the dance floor, you feel so good in my arms."

"One hour until - May I spend the night holding you? I promise nothing more, unless you want more. ☺"

Ah jeez, my nerves are frazzled and I feel an actual ache between my legs. I also feel nauseous; maybe this is a huge mistake. I've never felt this way. I could say I'm not feeling well; it's true so I wouldn't be fibbing. *Breathe Lisa, breathe.* He says if *you* want to, he isn't going to force himself on you. He wants to hold you all night long, which sounds wonderful, but oh so terrifying. *Why God?* Why does being with someone have to be so tempting? Is that what you want for me? Wayne? Is he the one I give myself to? Heart, soul, and *body*? I've waited twenty-four years for the right man, is Wayne the one? Tonight? Nah, this is only our second date. The

Turbulent Passion

weeks on the phone and texting don't count. *Be strong, Lisa.*

Okay, showered, lotioned, and dressed. Hair? Leave it long and sexy. Men like long hair. I must admit when I wear it straight it feels like silk.

Lucy will be proud I'm wearing make-up, a tiny bit of brown eye shadow with a pink highlight to bring out my green eyes, along with some pale pink blush and pink lip gloss, no biggie. I do think I need another coat of mascara and perfume. Where did I pack my perfume? "Dazzling Silver," by Estee Lauder, my absolute favorite. Men stop me on the plane all the time and ask what I'm wearing. Women everywhere should be thanking me for their gifts of "Silver." All I need to do is slip on my heels and I am ready.

My phone's beeping. Where did I leave it? I hear it. The sound is from my bed. There it is, under my panties. *How appropriate, Wayne in my underwear. Yea, yea, I know – focus.* The text reads, "Downstairs, aching to hold you, hurry!" *Alright, breathe Lisa and have fun.*

G.L. Ross

The elevator doors open inside the hotel lobby where Wayne stands wearing a pair of Wrangler jeans like no one's business and a tight fitting navy blue t-shirt that shows every ripped, rippled muscle in his chest. *It should be illegal to look so studly.* The navy blue brings out Wayne's intense dark blue eyes and whoa look at his arms. I didn't notice how muscular and strong they were in Galveston. I want those babies around me. *Slow down, Lisa. Whoooaaa Nellie.*

I lick my lips and take a deep breath before stepping out of the elevator. "Hi Wayne, you look great."

Wayne sweeps me into his arms, in a huge bear hug, and twirls us in a circle, before whispering in my ear, "Not nearly as great as you look and feel." *I knew the silk would work; he's already rubbing up and down my back.* Wayne kisses me as a man kisses a woman he wants to devour *or at least like it looks in the movies.* "Now I can make it to dinner. Lisa, you have no idea how I have missed you."

Turbulent Passion

"Oh, I think I have some idea." Can I get this silly grin off my face? *I look like the cat that ate the canary.*

Dinner and the jazz music were absolutely incredible. Tex-Mex is the best! The Mexican restaurant also had wonderful, but powerful margaritas. To say I am feeling no pain or insecurities is an understatement. *I am full of liquid courage.* Walking down 6th street towards the Country Western bar, Wayne has his arm securely around my waist, probably to make sure I don't trip and face plant on the street. *I really am feeling no pain.* I wish I liked beer. Wayne has been drinking Shiner beer, *the "Official beer of the great state of Texas."* Beer doesn't hit you as hard as tequila. I should have only had one margarita, rather than two. Honestly, I didn't realize Wayne ordered the second one and *I didn't want to waste it.* Walking will help sober me and the night air feels really good. I'll breathe deeply and hopefully my head will clear in no time. *I need to stay in control.*

"Here we are Lisa, best CW music in Austin." The band I hear playing is pretty good. The

G.L. Ross

best entertainment in Austin is people watching. There's a unique blend of cultures and personalities here. The people are passionate, talented, and creative. *What an eclectic group of people, no wonder the Austin motto is "Keep Austin Weird."*

Wayne locates a table towards the middle of the bar and orders another Shiner. I insist on water for me. "Come on Lisa, let's dance." *Okay, can this guy get any better?* A man who likes to dance…*Score!* I've never had a man take the lead like Wayne. I treasure the way he holds me tight and leads me in the two-step. He pushes me out, twirls me under his arm and pulls me back into his tight grasp. I feel like Cinderella, at the ball, when the Prince asks her to dance and leads her onto the floor.

Wayne makes me woozy *or is it the tequila?* He's strong and dominant, but then he is sweet, caring, and gentle. The problem is I truly cannot think clearly in his presence. I'm normally in control of my thoughts and decisions. I'm really not sure I like the idea of relinquishing control, to Wayne or any other man, especially when due to pheromones and hormones.

Turbulent Passion

When the music transitions to a ballad Wayne pulls me in close and nuzzles my neck. *Attention men! Nuzzling a woman's neck is a major turn on. My engine is revving.*

"Lisa, you mesmerize me. I wish you lived here, so we could see each other all the time."

"You would tire of me, Wayne. I think the distance makes you want me more." I bat and lower my long, dark lashes. *I'm using all of my tricks tonight. Yes, I am aware I don't have many. Give me a break. I am a novice.*

His long fingers lift my chin so I am gazing into Wayne's storm filled eyes as his raspy voice expertly seduces me, "I couldn't want you more than I do right now." Wayne presses his lips to mine, parting my lips with his persistent tongue he deepens the intensity of our kiss. His hands tug my waist and hips firmly against his torso. I feel his urgency to have me. As the music ends Wayne pulls his lips from mine and whispers, "Let me pay the bill and let's head back to the hotel."

G.L. Ross

Oh my, I need air, I need guidance, and I need a clear head.

"Okay, I will wait outside."

What, what, *what* am I going to do? He wants me. I want him. *But, it is waaayyy too soon.* I feel like I have known him forever *or okay at least a year* and I want to know him even better. He wants to know every *inch* of me. *Isn't that a good thing?* You want a man to desire you, to find you attractive. I've never had a man want me. Wayne awakens every nerve ending in my petite, *dormant* body. *Breathe Lisa, breathe.*

Our journey to the hotel was quietly and modestly filled with passion. There was a bunch of hand holding, hands caressing thighs, and intense gazes, but that was all. Right now I'm thankful there are other people in the elevator with us. The heat radiating between us could generate enough energy for all of Texas.

Wayne cuts his eyes and in a deep, smooth tone asks, "Which way is your room?"

Turbulent Passion

"To the left, room #442, here is the key." My hands are trembling, along with my voice, as I hand him the key card. The tension hanging in the air between us is wreaking havoc on my nerves. *I need a shot of whiskey, desperately.*

Wayne slips the key card in the lock and opens the door. "Ladies first."

"Thank you, sir. Wayne we -" *Oh shit!* Wayne stops and places his index finger against my lips.

Backing me against the wall he begins his skilled seduction. "Shh, no more talking. Only kissing." Wayne kisses my lips, my cheek, my ear lobe, my neck, *his tongue is very talented by the way,* oh there is that tingle again and that ache between my legs. I wish that ache would go far away. His talented, tantalizing tongue, *I love alliteration, I know – focus*, re-enters my mouth as his fingers begin unbuttoning my blouse. *Do I want this?* I think I do, but two dates?

His fingers trace the top of my bra brushing against the baby soft skin at the swell of my breasts. I

G.L. Ross

breathe deeply as my breasts rise to a tender trail of kisses across my sensitive cleavage. Biting through the lace of my bra, Wayne slips my nipple between his teeth and gently nibbles my taut peak. Oh my gracious, this is electric, what is happening to me? I feel a moist feeling developing between my legs. *What is happening to me?* Lucy is right. *I am naïve.*

Wayne slips my hand in his and leads me to the edge of the mattress. "Lisa, you are gorgeous," he soothes in his whiskey smooth sound. His deep tone spurs a need I wasn't even aware I possessed. Wayne sits on the edge of the king size bed, pulling me to stand between his powerful thighs. Grabbing hold of my curvy hips he pulls me toward him tracing his tongue across my bare stomach. He pauses a moment to tug his t-shirt over his head. *Goodness gracious he is built!* His gorgeous, toned, muscular chest is breath taking. I gasp for air. *Literally he has left me breathless.*

He loosens the button on my jeans, *oh God, what am I to do?* As he begins unzipping them I finally find the breath to speak, "Wayne, please wait." I place my hand on top of his.

Turbulent Passion

"What's wrong Lisa?" He stands to face me. Looking at his chest I find the nerve to say, "I'm not ready." *I said it. Whew...danger averted.*

"If you're worried about protection I have that covered." *What?* I hadn't really thought about that, since I am on the pill to regulate my periods and wasn't planning on being that intimate, but it is good to know he comes prepared, STD's and all, *or is that good?* Does that mean he has sex often? With lots of ladies? "Lisa, you okay? Look at me," he commands. I lift my head to look in his eyes. His eyes are so seductive, *but why am I seeing Lance? Damn you Lance...leave...now!* "Lisa?"

"No, I mean yes. I mean- please slow down." I want to scream. He makes me so confused. *Men are so confusing.*

"Sure baby, we can take this as slow as you like." He brushes my hair behind my shoulder. "I just want to be with you and kiss every sweet inch of you." While licking my ear he gravelly whispers, "I want to be inside you. Don't you want me inside you?" He leans back devouring me with his eyes. His stormy blue eyes are now black with desire. *Oh, dear*

G.L. Ross

Lord, what have I gotten myself into? I have to tell him. He'll understand. It won't frighten him away. He'll respect me and know that when I do let him 'kiss every sweet inch' of me he is the one. Whispering my name against my lips he begs for an answer, "Lisa?"

Just say it, Lisa! "I'm a virgin." I matter-of-factly say the words while looking at the floor *as though I am in trouble.* I should be proud that I have waited, that I have followed my beliefs and stood by my morals, but right now I feel like a child admitting to bad behavior.

"What?" Wayne is shocked and his voice holds an undercurrent of anger. "Did you say virgin?" I think the undercurrent is about to become a full-fledged storm.

Embarrassed I whisper, "Yes." My eyes still remain glued to the floor. Why do I feel as though I am in the principal's office? *Which I never went to, by the way.*

"Oh my God, Lisa! How old are you? You have never had sex?" *Okay, he is not taking this well.*

Turbulent Passion

Continuing to stare at the floor, I dig deep within for the strength to state, "I wanted to wait to 'make love', with my husband, not just have 'sex.'"

Wayne jerks his t-shirt back over his head and tucks it into his jeans. Pacing around the room nervously rubbing his hands through his jet black hair Wayne erupts, "But, I am not your husband."

"I know that Wayne." Now, I am getting angry. "I'm confused. I feel things with you, for you that I've never experienced. I just don't know that it is enough to "be" with you - like that." I feel the heat intensifying in my cheeks. I want to run in the bathroom and cry. Why did I stop him? It probably would have been better, less painful, and definitely less embarrassing if I had let him make love to me; but, that is the problem, he would not have made love to me, it would have been sex, just sex. I want more than that! *I deserve more than that.*

I gather my courage. While looking him directly in the eyes I walk towards him, with fierce determination. *I am Woman!* "Wayne, you act like you are mad at me for waiting, for standing by my beliefs. Are you mad at me, for being a virgin?"

G.L. Ross

"No, I am not mad." His voice softens as he takes a deep breath and blows it out, "I am shocked."

"I understand." I am shocked by all these roller coaster feelings coursing through me.

"Lisa, not many women in their mid to late twenties are virgins. Hell, you may be the only one."

"I guarantee you Wayne I am not in the Guinness Book of World Records as the oldest living virgin!" *Earth open up and take me now. Please!*

"I know that." Snickering Wayne wraps his arms around me holding me tightly against his muscular chest. "I'm sorry I reacted like I did, but that was a first for me."

"Well, it was almost a first for me." *Now that was funny*, we both laugh and enjoy the comment. Wayne kisses me lightly on the lips. He begins to pull away but I reach up and bring his head back. I kiss him allowing my tongue to explore his mouth and taste. I take charge. I am in control. First he seems to hold back, he wants to be in charge, but eventually he gives in molding his body to mine. I

Turbulent Passion

relax in his embrace. Whew, there is my Wayne, maybe I haven't lost him.

"Lisa, you are full of surprises," he smolders as his blue eyes burn through me.

"Yes I am and hopefully you feel I am worth the wait." I search his eyes for an answer.

"I guess that depends on how long the wait is." *Oh no, you didn't just say that!*

I slap his chest. "Hey, just teasing, walk me to the door. I think it is safe to say I am going to my own bed tonight." Wayne drapes his arm around my shoulder as we stroll to the door.

"I hope you really do understand." I search his eyes again hoping to find compassion.

Wayne leans his back against the open door and gathers me against him. Once again he expertly lures me into his arms. He rubs the back of his hand down my cheek. I shiver from the surprisingly tender touch. His eyes do not show understanding, but rather a raw hunger. Softly he presses his lips to mine, as our mouths part he softly speaks while staring

G.L. Ross

wolfishly into my eyes, "Lisa Price, there is passion inside of you dying to be released. You and I will release it - very soon. In fact, you will beg me to help you release it."

Wayne walks away as I continue to lean against the door jamb attempting to catch my breath and find any feeling still existing in my legs. *My legs are frickin' jelly, all rubbery.* His voice, eyes, mannerisms, and actions are all polar opposites. He is so damn confusing. *Men! I want to scream!*

"Well now, aren't you a sight for sore eyes." *Are you kidding me?* I wince as I recognize the ultra-sexy, caressing voice.

Exasperated I inhale deeply before responding, "Seriously, not you, not tonight." In front of me stands Captain America checking into a room across the hall from mine. *From mine! Really, God? Give me a break!*

"You seem to be breathing rapidly Miss Price. Are you okay?" Wipe that smirk off your face or I will wipe it off for you. You do not want to test me tonight.

Turbulent Passion

Life *and especially men* are entirely too complicated.

I decide to ignore Lance and his smug smirk. I enter my room, without uttering a word, allowing the door to close and lock behind me. *Admit it Lisa, you are naïve when it comes to men. But, I will not relinquish control or admit defeat. It is time I, Lisa Price, learn how to manage and control the male species.*

Watch out world...here comes the new, improved Lisa Price.

G.L. Ross

Turbulent Passion

Chapter Nine

Flyboy

Who was the fucker messing with my Goddess? I hurl my bag across the room and pace the floor searching for something to hit. There is absolutely no way I'm letting this slide. Continuing to pace within the confines of this incredibly small hotel room, I loosen and remove the constraint of my tie. Who was he and what was he doing in her room? *Hell, you know why he was in her room.* I unbutton my cuffs and remove my white dress shirt as I stare at the door to my room. She is across the hall from me, *right across the hall*, all hot and bothered and not by my seduction.

"She is *my* Goddess," I scream.

I sound like a damn child. Don't stand here whining you idiot! *Hurry up, change clothes, and go get her.*

Why am I standing in this smelly-ass hall freaked out and nervous? Knock on her door and invite her for a drink, damn it. *Stop standing here and knock before someone sees you.* I'm acting like a kid

G.L. Ross

meeting my date's father for the first time. *This is why I don't date. "Hit and Go" is so much easier, no drama.*

Knock on the damn door, Lance. My knuckles tap the door three times. She better answer quickly or else I'm outta here.

"Who is it?" I know she sees me through the peep hole.

"It's Lance. Open the door, Lisa."

"Go away Lance. I'm beat. I'm going to bed." *Not without me you're not.*

I brace one hand on the door and lean in closer. "Lisa, I am not leaving until you open this door."

"Guess it is going to be a long night then."

Shit. I slam the door with my fist. She is so damn frustrating. "Lisa, I am going to tap on this door until you open it." Tap, tap, tap, tap, tap…

"What?" She opens the door with her eyes half green and half black, her cheeks are flushed and

Turbulent Passion

her hair is long, straight, and silky. It takes everything in me to not sweep her in my arms and carry her to bed. I would kill to bury my hands in her golden locks. *I would love to bury other things inside her, too.*

"Thank you for opening the door." *Down boy.* Someone downstairs is eager to play.

Lisa sharply counters, "You didn't give me much of a choice."

Let me tell you, Miss Price has one hell of a curvaceous figure in her tight, white jeans. *And, check out the heels.* I would love to have those "come fuck me's" wrapped around my ass or flying spread eagle in the air.

Focus Lance, remember she despises you. You are here to win her over.

"You seemed a bit frazzled. Come downstairs and let me buy you a drink."

She begins to close the door. "I have already had my quota of alcohol for the night." I slap my hand against the door forcing it to remain open. Her

G.L. Ross

eyes open wide with shock and… *fear. Fear? Me? I would never hurt you intentionally, Lisa. You are my Goddess. I have searched for you for over half of my life.*

Think Lance, think. "Then have some water with me while I have a beer. My crew is slam-clicking and I would love your company." *That's good, go for the sympathy.*

"Lance really, I don't think…"

"Stop thinking." I push the door wide open, fly by her, and locate her key on the bedside table as I continue, "That's your first mistake." I grab the key, toss Miss Price over my shoulder, and kick the door closed. I simply won't allow her a choice or time to think. "Now, that's better." I place her feet on the hallway floor, wrap my arm around her enticingly small waist, and lead her towards the elevator. Miss Price is speechless. *That's a first.* Lisa's enticing mouth is open, but no words are escaping. *Mmm, I would love to slip my tongue in between those pouty, open lips.*

Turbulent Passion

"Excuse me…what, on earth, do you think you are doing?" she grunts while adjusting her clothing.

"Hijacking you for a visit, Miss Price," I proudly grin.

Upon entering the elevator, Lisa immediately chooses to stand on the opposite side from me and refuses to make eye contact by staring at the floor. *She is obviously not happy with my kidnapping technique.* I, on the other hand, can't help but stare and admire how absolutely beautiful my Goddess is, especially the way her anger illuminates her coloring. Lisa is vibrant and alive, full of energy and spunk, exactly the way I want her to always be when around me. The elevator doors open, without giving her a moment to think, I grab her hand and lead her towards a corner table in the hotel bar.

"May I take your order, sir?" The efficient waiter asks.

"Yes, a beer, whatever domestic that's on tap and a large glass of water for my friend." Lisa

G.L. Ross

snaps her gaze to mine displaying her disdain that I ordered for her.

Matter of factly I inquire, "Now Lisa, who was the man leaving your room tonight?" If looks could kill she just killed me twenty times.

"I had a date tonight and he walked me to my room, not that it is any of your business."

"Looked like he more than walked you to your room. You seemed a bit frazzled to me. Is he your boyfriend?" Lisa's lids lower while her hands nervously twist the cloth napkin on the table.

"No, not really." *Not really, but you were about to give it all up to him.* "We've gone out a few times." Her eyes lift to mine. "Lance, this really isn't any of your business." *Hell yes it's my business. You belong to me...M-i-n-e, mine.*

"Not true, Lisa. You are my business." Well, I think I grabbed Goddesses attention. Her eyes are as big as Texas. "I told you at breakfast that we were going to be friends *and lovers.*"

Turbulent Passion

The waiter arrives with our beverages. The electricity intensifies and sparks between us as we sit in silence gazing into each other's tumultuous eyes.

"See this time I made sure you had nothing to spit, sputter, or spill when I mentioned being your lover." I can't help but smile as Lisa fights her curving lips. "Now grab your glass Lisa, so we may make a toast - to us. Don't you dare roll your eyes at me, Miss Price." *Be careful barking orders. She's not yours, yet.* Calming my bark I continue, "Here's to us becoming friends and a whole lot more."

Lisa places her napkin in her lap before returning her eyes to mine. "I will toast to friends, but nothing more."

"I will take that as a start, my dear." As we toast our glasses I reach with my free hand to clasp hers. By the look in her eyes, I can tell she too feels the energy between us whether or not she chooses to admit it. Her look tells me she harbors a dark desire, for me. She wants me as much as I want her. *Well, perhaps not exactly as much, but close. I just know it.*

G.L. Ross

What is it about her? Is it her beauty? Her eyes? Her smile? No, it isn't purely physical. She challenges me. She holds her own. She doesn't throw herself at me. Is that it? Is it because she doesn't want me? *No, she does want me.* I've dreamt of this woman for years. Someone placed her vision in my dreams. She is meant to be mine. We belong together. *She just doesn't realize it, yet.* We were destined for each other. First though, I have to gain her trust as a friend.

"Lisa, what does that guy have that I don't? You agreed to a date with him. What must I do to convince you to give me a chance?"

That was kinda sappy, Lance. I think you're sinking to a new low for this gal. But, I want her to trust me, to need me, to think of me fondly rather than with disgust. I want her in my arms and in my bed, so first I have to reel her in, by being her friend.

Now, the question is, how does a guy become friends with a gal without having sex? I've never understood how that concept works. If I like a gal enough to hang with her then I want to bang her, and as soon as possible.

Turbulent Passion

With a lift of her left eyebrow, Lisa asks, "Do you really want me to answer that?"

"Yes, what do I need to do?" I sincerely request.

"Lance, you're not a boyfriend kind of guy. You're a 'flyboy.' You want a gal in every port, so to speak." The hairs on the back of my neck begin to raise their fighting fists.

I respond quickly and defensively, "And you think that guy doesn't have a different girl each night you are gone?" *Oops, I think I pissed her off.*

"No, I don't! He respects me. He respects women, which is more than I can say for you!"

"Lisa, you are looking for a fairytale. Fairytales are lies we tell ourselves about love. You, missy, need to stop being so naïve."

G.L. Ross

"Naïve?" she screams while tossing her napkin to the table. Her eyes shoot daggers at me as she enunciates, "I. Am. Done."

Lisa races to the elevator. "Lisa, stop," I holler. *Shit.*

I toss some cash on the table and hurry after her. I catch a glimpse of her as the elevator doors close. She is pissed. Fortunately, the other elevator arrives seconds after hers departs. Hurriedly I punch our floor. *Why did I push her so far? Calling her naïve is obviously a mistake.*

The elevator doors open and I see Lisa a couple of feet ahead of me. She can't travel expeditiously in those "come fuck" me heels, *thank goodness*. "Lisa, stop." I grab her bicep as she approaches her door. "You make me so angry," Lisa wails while pounding her fists against my chest. "I can't think or form intelligent sentences around you. You are everything I despise in men." I wrap my hands around her dainty wrists and push her back the length of my arms, to prevent her strikes. To be so

Turbulent Passion

petite she can sure pack a punch. "Just leave me alone. Stay out of my life." Doors begin to open as people hear our raised voices. I quickly release one wrist and slide her key card in the door, which thankfully is still in my possession. I enter her room yanking her in behind me as she continues her verbal assault screaming, "Get out of my room!"

"No! Not until you hear me out," I bark.

"I'm calling security."

I am sure they are already on their way with all your howling.

Simultaneously, I reach for her arm as she reaches for the phone. Tangled in our struggle for control we both lose our balance falling upon the bed - with Goddess landing on top of me. *I must say for an unplanned action it sure turned out sweeeet!* The feel of Goddesses' voluptuous body against mine is extraordinary. The few minutes we remain frozen on the bed are the best minutes of my life, so far.

G.L. Ross

Entranced by her beauty it takes me a few minutes before I notice her spellbinding eyes are actually blazing with desire, but only for a split second. Once she feels my chub she immediately jumps to her feet shouting, "Get off of me."

"Hate to break it to you sweetheart, but you were on top off me." *Miss Price is fuming and I am so turned on I can't stand it.* I return to my feet, rearrange myself, and mosey my way to grab a seat near the desk. "Lisa, calm down and let's visit - please." I flash her my best puppy dog eyes.

She inhales a deep breath and I swear she counts to ten, before sitting on the edge of the bed. The phone rings, she answers and explains to the front desk that security will not be required. *Whew, escaped that one.*

After hanging up the phone, Lisa returns to sit on the edge of the bed. "Why do you enrage me? I never speak to people in such a rude, ugly way, but you - you release this animalistic rage in me. I explode uncontrollably when near you. You really need to stay away from me, Lance." She stands and

Turbulent Passion

walks towards the door. With a hand resting on the door knob, she turns and request, "Please leave."

I walk towards her and notice her shoulder's begin to relax. She thinks she has won and I am leaving. Instead I tip her chin upwards with my fingers. Focusing on her emerald gems I calmly and matter-of-factly explain, "I don't care if you scream at me, spit at me, or sleep with me. I. Want. You. In. My. Life. However I can have you." Her startled eyes transfix and for the first time I see heat, not anger heat, but sex heat, from Miss Price, directed towards me, wanting me and for more than a split second.

I gently place my free hand on her lower back and push her hips against mine. She lightly gasps parting her lips ever so slightly. Still holding her chin I place my lips lightly against hers, without closing my eyes I deepen the kiss. At first she hesitates, but as my tongue traces her lips she sighs, closes her eyes, and relinquishes control to me. I jump at the opportunity and slide my tongue into her warm, sweet mouth. She begins to pull away so I slide my hand behind her head lacing my fingers into those sought after golden strands. Lisa is trapped,

G.L. Ross

finally, unable to leave my arms. *She can't leave me.*
I have her. *In my arms.* On my lips. *She is mine.* If
only for a few minutes.

My body grows hotter for her with each
passing second. *After twenty years of imagining this
moment my dream has come true and it is even better
than I dreamt it would be.* My hand placed on her
lower back slides downward to cup her firm cheek.
The apples are as sweet as I imagined. I hold her
tightly against my bulging crotch. She doesn't fight
me. She willingly tilts her head so I may continue to
lick and savor her taste. She allows me the
opportunity to own her mouth. Her fingers slide up
my chest igniting a fire smoldering inside me. I back
her against the wall, grab her leg, and wind it around
my hips. The feel of her thigh transitioning to her
curvaceous ass sends me spiraling.

I lose control as her fingers inch into my
hair. I lift her bottom wrapping both of her legs
around my waist. While carrying her to the bed I
push my expanding bulge against her wet, heat
soaked jeans. *Miss Price is definitely aroused.* My
tongue licks and tastes her neck, her chest, her cheek.

Turbulent Passion

She moans and I have to own her. With one hand I unzip my jeans as I lower our entwined bodies to the bed. My eyes continue to absorb the heat radiating from my Goddess as I unbutton my unzipped jeans. I push my jeans over my hips until I see fear replacing the heat in Lisa's emerald eyes.

"What? What's wrong Lisa?" I cup her sweet face in my hands while placing a soft kiss on her lips. Her body tenses as she begins to shake her head.

She rolls away from me. "Leave. Please leave," she softly chokes. My Goddess is trembling, seriously shaking with fear. "I can't. I won't. I'm sorry I lead you on," she expresses through choked back tears.

"Lisa you didn't lead me on, you wanted me. You felt it between us." My hand clutches her shoulder. I gently ease her back against my chest. My arms wrap around her waist. I bury my face in her hair. *She smells so good.* Her entire body is as tight as a bow string. "Don't be afraid of me Goddess. I will never force myself on you. I'm crazy about you," I whisper against her hair. Under my breath I mumble,

G.L. Ross

"You make me want to be a better man. I'll wait until you are ready. I will wait for you, Lisa."

"Don't Lance. Don't wait for me." After deeply inhaling her incredible scent, I lift my face and see tears staining her rosy cheeks.

"What is wrong, Lisa? Please tell me."

"Leave, Lance. Please," she whimpers. I place a kiss on the top of her head while continuing to hold her in my arms.

"One day Lisa you will trust me. I promise you I will earn your trust."

Goddess

"What the hell was that?" Seriously? I go from no men in my life to two men in one night trying to get in my pants! This is out of control.

Lance must have left after I fell asleep - in his arms. It was nice being held against his warm, strong, spicy scented, muscular body. How long did I snooze? Crap, it's 3 AM.

Turbulent Passion

I quickly grab my shower stuff and head into the bathroom. I need to take a shower, a cold shower, and get my butt to bed. In the morning, *well technically it is already morning,* I will try to decipher all of the testosterone flowing my way. *Jeez, Louise.*

"Shit! That is cold!" *Note to self, test water before stepping in.* That definitely takes the heat out of all extremities. No wonder guys take so many cold showers.

I switch to hot water to shampoo my hair and wash my face, while scrubbing with apricot exfoliator and conditioning my hair I consider both *controlling* men. Wayne is who I need to stick with. Yes, he was pissed, but I surprised him. He respects me, whereas Lance is an A#1 player, who merely wants to add me to his list of bountiful conquests. He doesn't want to be my friend. *He wants to be my friend with benefits!*

I slip under the down comforter and crisp sheet emotionally drained. I set my alarm clock, turn off the lights, and recite my prayers, "Lord, please guide me. These men are way too confusing. Do I

G.L. Ross

want either of them? " I begin to drift off to la-la land, with both men's faces popping into my dream. As I am falling into a deep sleep a thought enters my mind, "Did Lance call me 'Goddess'?"

****

The next few weeks Wayne and I spent talking on the phone. I was unable to get an Austin overnight, which is probably best since we need to get to know each other intellectually and not just physically. We definitely are attracted to each other, but as we delve into deeper topics, such as faith, family, and marriage, we seem to have differing views. Wayne's parents divorced when he was a teen-ager and the idea of marriage, being a life time commitment, seems to terrify Wayne, *of course he would never admit it*. He appears to like kids, but as long as they are someone else's and not crying. What really concerns me is his faith. Last night, as we were talking on the phone, I invited him to come to Dallas and attend church with me, "Wayne we have a wonderful contemporary service with a band that plays Pop/Rock Christian music. You may even wear jeans to the service, which begins at 6:00 on Saturday

Turbulent Passion

night. I am off and was hoping you would fly here and go with me. You may stay with me at my apartment."

"Lisa, I don't do the church thing. That is really not my deal." Not his deal?

"You are a Christian right? You wear a ring with a cross on it." *Please be a Christian.*

"My mom gave me that as a Christmas gift one year. I'm not sure I am a Christian. I'm 'Spiritual.'" *Seriously? Spiritual?*

"Spiritual? What exactly does that mean, Wayne?" I'm not sure if I'm sad, scared, or angry. *I need help here, Lord.*

"I believe there is a God and that each of us can find an inner peace, in our own individual way."

"Oh." I think my heart just broke. He believes there is a God, which is good; but not necessarily my God, which is bad.

"Lisa, why don't you come here for the weekend? You can stay with me and I will even

G.L. Ross

make you dinner. You may ask me all the questions you want then, okay?"

I knew he seemed too good to be true, but maybe he needs to be introduced to Jesus and church. Everything else between us is really good besides as he falls in love with me he will join me for church services. I can make this work or am I trying to convince myself? I don't want to push him away or scare him. "Sure Wayne, I would love to come spend the weekend with you."

Turbulent Passion

Chapter Ten

Manwhore

The feel of her body against mine. My hands on her warm, lightly toasted skin. Her sweet taste on my lips. I love the way she became willing and excited to my touch. She's so damn stimulating. *I might as well face it, she is my drug and I am addicted.*

But, like a fool, I scared the shit out of her. She was trembling. Why did I come on so strong? *Show some restraint, man.* You were supposed to become her friend, not get her in bed the first time you were alone with her. Foreplay would have been plenty, *but hell no, I undo my pants!*

I have to stop pacing. I need to be deep inside her, with my face in her hair absorbing her vanilla scent. *Her scent is... maddening.* I can still smell her. I want my dick in her warm, tight tunnel. She was so wet, even through her jeans. *She wanted me, damn it.*

Now all I get is another night jerking off in the shower, *shit.*

G.L. Ross

My hands lay plastered against the shower wall as the hot water floods over my highly sensitized body. "God, come on. I am trying. *Let. Me. Have. Her.*" I cry.

****

Two days later I pick up an extra fly assignment with an overnight in Nashville, Tennessee; a quick and easy two day trip, with lots of time to play. My FO and I arrive in Nashville around 6 PM. We change clothes and head out to discover some of Nashville's outstanding country bars. There is fresh, innovative country music in Nashville. There are also incredible Southern women. *I need something to help me forget Lisa.*

My FO, Patrick, and I make the rounds enjoying wonderful music and women. I'm about to consider hooking up with a beautiful redhead when I run into one of the girls I savored about a month or two ago. She and her crew are climbing into a cab when she spots us.

"Hey handsome. Need a ride to the hotel?" she seductively purrs.

Turbulent Passion

Patrick and I smile and climb into the "land of opportunity." I squeeze boobalicious into my lap as we begin our ride to the hotel. "Hey sweetheart." *That's what I call them when I can't remember their name.* "Thanks for the ride." I tilt and thrust my pelvis against her ass. Leaning in I whisper, "Want to come to my room for a real ride?" Boobalicious places a hand on my thigh sliding it up to my crotch and smiles as she licks her lips. *I believe that was a yes.*

All five of us burst into the lobby laughing and hanging on each other. Boobalicious has her hand on my ass as I stare down into her hilly, abundant flesh. I raise my eyes to locate the elevator when I am face to face with fierce, raging emerald eyes.

Standing with her hands on her hips, as her co-workers hold the elevator for her, I am ripped a new asshole. "You manwhore! Trust you? Right! Do you take me for a fool? An idiot? I am naïve? *Not!* When was she? How was she? Women are absolutely disposable to you? Is your only requirement a vagina between spread eagle legs?"

G.L. Ross

I hear everyone's gasps and snickers as I drop my arm from boobalicious and mentally register the run-on verbal assault spewing from Lisa. *Quite honestly I forget everyone else is there witnessing our tumultuous exchange.*

"You are driving me fucking crazy, Lisa! I have never wanted anyone like I want you. You have taken over my mind, for the love of God, but you send me all kinds of mixed messages. Last I heard you despised me."

Snarkily Lisa attacks, "I have taken over your mind? But not your body and that is your real issue and apparent need, at all times, seven days a week, twenty-four hours a day. So rather than abstain to prove your sincerity you screw another bimbo blond."

The blond glares at Lisa and begins a rebuttal, until I push her back towards Patrick. Lisa continues her head-on assault, "That is supposed to prove your love and faithfulness to me? I am supposed to be okay with this because she means nothing to you? You are unbelievable, Lance," she

Turbulent Passion

snorts before turning to enter the elevator with her crew.

"Well, that I am," I humbly agree.

I am unbelievable in bed, so I have been told – numerous times.

Storming off in a frustrated huff I chase after her. "Give me a chance to explain."

Standing inside the elevator holding the doors open, with her green eyes shooting daggers she asks, "Okay. Be honest. When did you screw her? Last night?"

"God no."

"Okay when?"

"A month or two ago, before we had our evening."

"You are really messed up." Lisa steps back allowing the doors to close while never removing her hurt-filled eyes from mine.

G.L. Ross

I suffer my own agony watching my dream Goddess leave me once again.

I return to my room alone and for about twenty minutes I pace and converse with myself. "Why is she pissed? She told me, 'No way, Jose'. She said I enraged and confused her. So why is she ticked off?" She exploded. She royally lambasted me.

I splash cold water on my face and stare into the mirror searching for an answer that makes sense. Ten minutes later it hits me…she wants me! She really wants me. *It ate her up seeing me with someone else. Hot damn!* I have to see her. We have to talk.

I hurry downstairs to check the crew list. I can find out what room Lisa is in from the sign in sheet. I approach the lobby and hear a wave of laughter coming from the bar. *Maybe?* Maybe my luck has changed and Goddess is unknowingly waiting for me in the bar.

Turbulent Passion

Virgin

Why on earth did I lose it like that? Who cares if he is with another one of his bimbos? I don't. *So why did I get so angry?* Every time I see him I overreact. The man truly brings out the bitch in me.

Let it go. *Let him go.* Breathe Lisa, take a deep breath, count to ten, and exhale. Release the frustration and head downstairs for a fun, relaxing crew debrief.

Laughter, fun, and several alcoholic beverages will erase Lance from my bewildered mind. *So, why does that thought somewhat disturb me?*

I continue tormenting myself by replaying the lobby scene in my mind. I detest losing control. Usually I am a strong, self-assured woman, which is another reason to steer clear of Lance; I lose my true self when with him. I need to remember this feeling and how disgusted I am with myself, so I never allow it to happen again.

G.L. Ross

Un-frickin'-believable, I am once again in an elevator and have no recollection of walking to it or entering it. *I seriously have to get a grip.*

"Lisa, over here," my crew yells and motions me to join their laughter filled table.

"What may I get you to drink, mam?" The waitress doesn't appear to be old enough to serve alcohol.

"White wine, whatever type is on special." My thought is interrupted as Jack pulls up a chair to the table for me.

"We are very happy that you chose to come join us," Martha shares while giving me a side-ways hug.

Julie chimes in, "I'm happy you are here, but aren't you afraid you will run into him?"

Martha kicks Julie under the table, before I have a chance to reply. "Martha leave Julie alone. I appreciate your concern Julie, but he is on an AM so I am sure he is climbing into his bed right now." *Stop*

Lisa; stop thinking of him naked in bed. I am making myself crazy.

Another crew joins our party and the laughter continues to build. After a second glass of wine and an hour of bust a gut howling I am completely over my emotional tirade. Of course, completely forgetting Lance will take a bit longer.

"Julie how is your shin? I can't believe Martha kicked you."

"It's okay. I've had worse hits from turbulence on the plane," she states while rubbing her shin.

"That is a true statement indeed." We giggle obnoxiously due to our consumption of wine. My laughter is over the top, due to drinking before eating. *Not a smart move.* But, when my nerve endings begin to tingle and my flesh begins to heat I know it is not because of the alcohol. My body recognizes his presence. I don't see him. I don't need to, I know. My senses heighten. I inhale his earthy, cinnamon spice scent. Teetering on the edge of reason I turn my head towards the bar entrance. His hungry gaze greets my

G.L. Ross

confused, awestruck ogling. This man wreaks havoc on my life, yet I melt at the sight of his enticing muscular physique and bold, demanding stance. Lance blatantly commands the room and the women in it. Every woman in this room is undressing and fucking him in their mind. They're imagining the scintillating touch I have experienced. An aching dampness lingers between my legs. *Why does he affect me this way?* No words are spoken or required. Our eyes say all that needs to be said. There is an intimacy between us, which I vehemently know is wrong. *Yet, I want him...badly.*

My crew turns to see what or who has captured my attention. One of the pilots offers to intervene and ask Lance to leave, but I don't want anyone else involved in our turmoil, especially a co-worker. "Lisa, you don't have to talk to him. Martha and I will leave with you and stay with you in your room until we know he is gone. We can even change rooms with you," Julie sweetly offers.

"Thanks Julie, but I can handle him." *Can I, really?* "I overreacted earlier. I need to make this wrong right."

Turbulent Passion

Lance continues to stand in the doorway beckoning me to join him. *Lisa, if you go with him you must be willing to accept the consequences of your actions.* I feel entranced. Reason has abandoned me. I place cash on the table and excuse myself. My legs quiver beneath me as I stand. I take one step towards him and stop. *Are you sure Lisa? You know how emotional and weak you become when with him.* My eyes lift and lock with his. His devilish, penetrating stare continues to draw my steps towards him. His fingers lace with mine when I reach him and for some bizarre reason I relax.

We enter the elevator, Lance pushes the button for our floor, and we watch the doors close. Silently we stand absorbing each other's heated appreciation and scrutiny. The bell dings, the doors open. I hand Lance my key card. Upon reaching my room he slides the card into the lock. Prior to opening the door he leans and whispers seductively in my ear, "We need to talk…first." *I am soaking wet.*

Shortly after we enter the room I hear the door close behind me. I nervously move towards the desk, attempting to get something, *besides a bed,*

G.L. Ross

between Lance and me. "Lance, I don't know why I…" Before I'm able to complete my sentence I feel Lance's warm breath feathering across my neck. His fingers stroke the length of my hair and across my bare shoulders, halting my word formation. I begin to lean my body, *even though I know I shouldn't*, into his touch. The stubble on his face brushes against my hypersensitive ear and into my hair. He inhales my "Dazzling" scent and moans initiating an aching fire throughout my body. *So this is how it feels to be ravished, devoured, perhaps loved.*

Lance pulls my back against his chest wrapping his sinewy arms around my waist; one hand spreads across my abdomen. His touch heats and excites my flesh. The blood rushing through my brain roars in my ears. Angel light kisses tingle across my skin. His fingers begin to move across my hips. I lift my arms up around his neck inviting him to explore my many curves. Slowly his hands begin to worship and memorize my body. *Why are there sparks with him, but no one else?*

Lance's deep, husky voice floats across my hair and neck, "Lisa, you have no idea how long I

Turbulent Passion

have wanted to feel your body willingly against mine, in my hands, ever since I first dreamt of you I have wanted you to be mine and only mine." I can't concentrate. All I can think about is how my breasts feel molding into his hands. My nipples harden from the brush of his thumbs. I arch my back pushing for his hands to claim all of me. *Pinch my nipples. Bite my neck. Take me, please take me.* His pelvis urges his growing manhood against my backside. *Breathe and relax Lisa, for once in your life don't analyze simply enjoy the moment.*

I try to convince the voice in my head to relax, to go with the moment, to enjoy the sensations and attention. *He's gorgeous. Go with it, girl.*

His hand moves down my stomach, across my sex, and between my legs. *Relax, Lisa relax.* Slowly his hands push aside my skirt and soaked panties. His fingers tease and taunt my engorged clit. His hips grind into me as his fingers slide through my wet heat. One finger slips inside me. I tense until Lance soothes my nerves with his whispers *and the palming of my left breast*. His finger continues to slide in and out of my abundant wetness, while his other hand squeezes and pinches my left nipple harshly. At first it hurts, but the pain quickly becomes pleasure. My mind argues between the sensations.

Lance slides a second finger inside me. My head falls back against his chest. My body tightens, my back bows, my sex clenches Lance's fingers. *What is happening?* My vision blurs. My pulse reverberates in my head. My entire body erupts. *So this is what an orgasm feels like? If so, again please.* I collapse into the security of Lance's strong, muscular arms. He continues to soothe me with his words while cradling me against his chest.

In one quick motion he repositions me so my legs wrap around his waist. He walks to where he can push me against a wall. This feels like a scene from a movie *and I am in it* and its frickin' hot and sexy. The tip of his tongue traces my ear before he groans, "I feel like a teenager rubbing myself against you." His hips urgently grind against me pushing his growing bulge into my soaked sex. "I want you, Lisa. I want to bury myself deep inside you." Lance slips his fingers back under the lace bathing his finger along my cleft. The feel of my extremely wet

Turbulent Passion

opening elicits a wild, skyrocketing response, in Lance. "God, I have to have you," he moans before crushing his mouth against mine. His fingers enter me. "I have to feel you come against my fingers, again." *God above could he be the man for me?*

My sex instinctively pushes into his hand. "These have to go," he heatedly grunts as he rips the lace of my panties and tosses them to the side. His thumb circles my clit as he plunges another finger inside me. "I want to fill you with all of me. I want my dick deep inside thoroughly fucking you, Lisa," he moans as his rock hardness pushes against my thigh. The intensity of his fingers and growing desire disrupt all logical thinking. I drop my head against his shoulder. Driving me up and up I feel myself tighten and arch into him before going limp in his arms. "There you go, baby."

Lance carries me to the bed cradled in his arms. His mouth engulfs my breast through the sheer fabric. He lifts his head and snickers.

"What?"

G.L. Ross

"The smile on your face, it's amazing." He returns the smile before biting my nipple.

"Hey," I snip. "Not so hard." He sucks and bites my nipple once again.

"Again, please," I sweetly request. He traps my nipple between his teeth and lifts his eyes to mine. "No," I sheepishly reply. Lance searches my darkened eyes. He recognizes my enjoyment and responds by growing harder against my hip. I smile and state, "Again, please." This time I lower my eyes to my hips.

I slide his hand between my legs. "Oh, so you liked that?" He smiles and asks. My face is fifty shades of red as I blush. I've never been so brazen. Of course, I've never allowed a man to touch me, like this.

I rise to kiss his cheek and whisper, "Oh yes." *See what happens when you relax and enjoy, Lisa.*

"You are wonderfully wet," Lance moans right before his mouth and fingers take me over the edge again. Sliding my mini-dress over my head

Turbulent Passion

Lance whispers against my lips, "I want to see all of you." Lance stands at the end of the bed drinking me in. "You are sensationally gorgeous."

I should be embarrassed, especially when you consider where his mouth has been, but I'm basking in the glow of the rush soaring through my body. He begins unbuttoning his jeans when I close my eyes. "Lisa, look at me." I open my eyes and watch as he unzips and lowers his jeans. I divert my eyes at a certain point, *although I would really like to stare and memorize the incredibly amazing view of his penis.*

"Lisa, Please." He bends to remove his jeans and I am amazed by his golden rippling muscles. He has pecs, biceps, triceps, lats, washboard abs, and a V that leads me to the glory land. When he stands straight my mouth gapes, my eyes freeze on the length and size of his pulsing, fully erect penis. My eyes display my shock and fear. *That is never going to fit.* Lance crawls and braces himself above me. His knees lower to rest between my spread thighs. His hands glide across my skin soothing my fears. Lowering himself against me he pants, "The feel of

G.L. Ross

your skin against my skin is explosive. Tell me you like it, too. Lisa, I have dreamed of this, of you and me together." He tenderly traces my lips with his tongue. My lips part as I sigh. Lance licks in and out of my mouth. The passion rekindles to full throttle. Lifting himself above me I feel the length of his penis sliding through my moisture-filled cleft. Staring into my eyes he reassures me, "Lisa, you will expand. I will fit. I would never intentionally hurt you. If it stings it will only be for a second."

"Yes, I know. I've read about it, but Lance I need to tell you something first."

His eyes search mine. He rolls to his side and props his elbow against the mattress elevating his head beside me. "What is it Lisa?" *Wow, that was easy.*

Lance's arms wrap around me. His warm hands massage the front of my body. I moan and mold my body to his. "Tell me Lisa. Do not be afraid to be honest with me." My hands drop to my sides massaging Lance's thighs and bottom. His thigh muscles tighten under my touch. I'm amazed a man reacts to my touch, so sensually. My hands slide

Turbulent Passion

towards Lance's inner thighs. He releases a guttural moan as he pulls me against him threading his legs with mine.

"I'm a virgin, Lance." I close my eyes waiting for the eruption and humiliation.

Lance's lips brush against mine. His knuckle slides down my cheek. "Lisa, open your eyes and look at me."

"No, it's embarrassing." I raise my hands to cover my face.

Lance removes my hands and commands me, "Open your eyes now, Lisa."

I lift my long, thick lashes and force my eyes to lock with his. Once again Lance hovers above me. "Lisa, you aren't telling me something I don't already know." *What?*

"How could you?" I ask.

Lance reaches for his jeans and grabs a condom. He rips the packet with his teeth and responds, "Lisa, your body's reaction to my touch

G.L. Ross

said what words didn't say. You would be nervous, but not terrified, if you had been with a man before. Plus, your reaction to your first orgasm was probably the best experience of my life." *It was the best experience of mine, for sure.* "It means everything to me to know I gave you your first orgasm and am about to be the first man to make love to you." *Wow. I believe he is a keeper.*

"You don't think I'm weird?"

Lance laughs before kissing me. "If you are weird, then you are my kind of weird. Now where were we?" Lance plunges his tongue inside my mouth tasting and licking, before sucking and teasing my tongue. His fingers explore my sex. His tongue tortures my erect nipples. My body arches against him. He pulls to his knees and I am impressed as he rolls the condom the length of his Herculean penis. It's so engorged; there are veins pulsing and protruding. *I did this. I caused this reaction. Me. Unreal.*

"Baby, relax and let me be in charge."

Turbulent Passion

For once in my life I am glad someone else is in control. My hands slide up Lance's rippling muscled arms as he rocks his penis gently against my swollen opening. I see Lance's struggle in his eyes. It means so much to me that he is concerned with my experience, more than his. He wants this to be enjoyable for me. A happy memory.

"Lisa, wrap your legs around me and anchor your feet against my ass. I'm going to slowly enter you, so try to relax." Before pushing into me, Lance engulfs my left breast in his warm mouth. I'm focused on the scintillating suction as Lance enters my tight tunnel. I gasp, but Lance quickly pushes deeper before trailing kisses up my neck. His hand slides under my hips angling me in order to delve deeper. "You are so tight baby. It's taking everything in me to not plunge all the way inside you. Lisa, baby, you feel good." I want him. I want him deep within me. My feet press against his cheeks encouraging him to plunge deeper. His eyes flash hungrily at mine. Lance inhales deeply, trying to maintain control. I tilt my hips and push my feet. My body pleads for all of him. "Greedy, are you? Does Lisa want all of Lance?" he teases.

G.L. Ross

I want to know what it feels like to have all of him pulsing inside me.

"Yes!" I urge. Lance lifts my hips and punctures all the way through my virginity. We both moan and cling together. I am speechless. Lance pauses a moment before beginning slow partially penetrating movements in and out of me. My slickness allows him to slide without pain. Pleasure builds as I find my hips responding automatically to his strokes.

"I love your sweet, tight grip. I've never felt anything like you, baby." My eyes sparkle. I, Lisa Price, make this gorgeous man feel extraordinary. Lance pushes to his knees and redirects his girth to rub against a spot that elicits a firework response between my legs. "Ride it, baby." I push into Lance's plunges. I love watching his hips roll as he slides all the way in and out of me. His desire grows as his speed increases. He repositions over me and wraps my legs around his hips. His chest hairs brushing against my nipples and his body rubbing against my engorged clit encourages my legs to wrap and hold him tighter. "Hang in there, baby. Are you almost

Turbulent Passion

there?" *Where?* "Are you about to cum, baby?" His eyes beg me for an answer.

"I think so. It feels so good, Lance." My response is all the encouragement he needs. His face buries into my neck as he moans and grunts while pounding into me. I hear the slapping of our glistening sweaty bodies. My body begins to tighten.

"That's it, Lisa. Squeeze me tight. Take all of my juices." I feel my sex clenching and squeezing his pulsing length and width. My body is being stretched and pulled so tightly. "Oh my God, Lisa. Now! Cum now!" The tightly wound bow releases its arrow. My entire body soars and slams against Lance's strong, sturdy frame.

A-ma-zing. Well worth the wait. I can't imagine having shared this with anyone but Lance.

Lance's trembling body falls upon mine and his warmth feels like home. *I think my arrow finally found its target.*

G.L. Ross

Turbulent Passion

Chapter Eleven

Adam

Did that really happen? Did I finally, physically and not mentally, make love to my Goddess? Hell yea!

I smile proudly as I gaze downward into her glossed over eyes, her flushed cheeks, and sexy bedhead hair. I did this. I caused her to experience the highest of highs. I helped her find peace, tranquility, joy. All by being in my arms.

"You okay, baby?" I lightly brush my lips across her shimmering forehead. I shove a pillow under my head while curling Lisa seamlessly to my side.

"Lisa, baby, you still with me?" I tease.

"Mmmhmm," she hums displaying a sated smile. My sleepy Goddess repositions her naked body placing her cheek over my heart, *which is exactly where she belongs.* I never thought anyone would hold a place in my heart quite like this. For the first time in my life, I am truly content, happy,

G.L. Ross

fulfilled. I realize the type of man I want to be. A man who spends the rest of his life honoring one woman, loving one woman, one Goddess. *Miss Price has claimed my heart.*

"You sleepy?" My fingers stroke her golden, tangled tresses as her hand snakes around my waist. Her breathing becomes deep and even. "Lisa?" She slides her leg between mine entwining our bodies. I wrap my dream Goddess securely against my side as she drifts into a dreamy, blissful sleep. As I feel her pulse against my ribs the story of Adam and Eve flashes across my mind. Eve came from Adam's rib. She was made for him, from a part of him. Lisa was made for me, *without a doubt*; she is a part of me. God placed her in my dreams years ago, so when faced with reality I would give real, honest, love a chance. He knew it would take being slapped in the face, before I would open my heart to someone. *Thank you. Thank you for your divine intervention and plan.* Thank you for giving me the desire of my heart, even before I realized it.

Turbulent Passion

"I know you're sleeping, baby, but I need to say this." My fingertips glide across the silky curvature of her bare back. Gently I pull the covers over us, careful not to wake her, as I continue, "I will always take care of you, Lisa." I delight in having her under my arm. Resting my chin on top of her head, I place a kiss on her crown. "I love you. I always have and I always will."

****

Where is that damn alarm? Turn it off. I slap my hand across the bedside table.

"Lance, answer it," Lisa groggily mumbles.

"Answer what, Lisa? It's the alarm." I'm warmly greeted by two voluptuous breasts plastered against my face as Lisa climbs over me to turn on the light.

"Hello," she answers the phone. *It was the phone ringing?* "Yes, I have a pen and paper." I decide to return the morning greeting by engulfing Lisa's left tit in my warm mouth. "Whaaat?" she screeches. Covering the phone she admonishes me, "It's Scheduling Lance, stop it." I smile, laugh, and continue teasing her nipple with my tongue, teeth, and lips. She scrunches her face at me and continues

G.L. Ross

to scribble information. "Yes, I will be there. Forward position, flight 224, got it. No problem, happy to help."

"Did you say flight 224, Lisa?"

Lisa glances at the clock prior to sliding her body seductively down mine, after hanging up the phone. She knows exactly what she is doing to me with each touch, with each tantalizing vibration.

"You were a bad boy. I was receiving information regarding an assignment change," she provocatively reprimands me. She sucks my ear lobe before nipping her way down my jawline. "It seems your forward flight attendant is ill so I am being switched to your trip." I feel the man downstairs standing at full attention and apparently Lisa is ready for his full attention, also. She brushes her lips against mine, before sitting up to lower herself onto my pulsing, thickening dick. She places my hands on each of her full, firm, heavy breasts. "Captain, would you mind sharing my bed again tonight in Fort Lauderdale?" *No one has ever looked more beautiful with unruly morning hair.*

Turbulent Passion

I push myself into a sitting position and wrap her delectable legs around my hips. I suck her hardened nipple before answering, "I do believe that can be arranged Miss Price. I didn't think my day could get any better than waking with you in my arms, but it just did." I thrust my hips upward causing Lisa to wince. My tongue darts into her mouth stroking and savoring her ever so sweet droplets. "We have fifteen minutes until we need to hit the shower – together," I grin.

Lisa brazenly smiles before sharing an Eskimo kiss. "Then you better get busy flyboy." *Yes, mam.*

Eve

"So, tell me Lance, how did you manage to arrange adjoining hotel rooms for us?" I inquire while backing him against a bedroom wall. I have no idea how to do what I am about to do, but I trust my urges and Lance's responses to guide me.

Lance gives me a curious, yet pleasantly surprised look. "I made a phone call earlier in the day."

G.L. Ross

"I don't know when you found time with all the beverages you requested I deliver to the cockpit, the restroom breaks to come visit me in the front galley, and then all the assistance you provided during boarding and deplaning," I coyly detail while removing his tie and starched white shirt.

I have to tell you - this man has the most gorgeous chiseled chest ever.

"You really shouldn't be allowed to wear shirts, Lance." My fingers explore each wave of his chorded chest and V. "It seems a crime to hide this magnificence from everyone's view."

Lance responds to me in an extremely intimate tone, "There's only one person's view I care about." I press my finger to Lance's lips, preventing him from kissing me. My exploring fingertips, tongue, and lips appreciatively trace the feel of his broad powerful chest, taut six pack stomach, narrow enticing hips, and tempting happy trail before lowering to my knees and taking his slacks and briefs with me. "Lisa, what are you doing?"

Turbulent Passion

"What does it look like flyboy?" I smile wickedly before my warm mouth welcomes his wide crown between my pouty lips. His knees slightly buckle when surrounded by my warmth. I deeply suck his tip and feel a rush as he cheers me on, "Exactly like that. Oh Lisa, yes, lick me baby. Suck me with that gorgeous mouth." His hands grasp and pull my hair as I cup his swollen balls. Greedily I consume his entire length inside my mouth and deep into my throat. I fist and jack his root as my tongue swirls, sucks, and teases his tip. His trembling, well-built thighs and shallow breathing motivate and energize me to pump his pleasure beyond his wildest imagination. I reach back near his weighty sacs and mouthwatering ass for the pressure point I've read men enjoy having pushed. Once I locate the spot Lance throws his head against the wall exhaling, "For the love of God you are my Goddess." My mind is boggled that I, naïve Lisa Price, can sexually please someone like Lance Miller, so intensely. His hands grasp my head as he plunders my mouth. I cling to his athletic thighs for stability. Eagerly I lick the salty pre-cum gleaming on his tip. "Suck me harder, baby," he instructs. "I love the way you enjoy tasting

G.L. Ross

me." His moans empower me. *But, can I handle it if he comes in my mouth?* I want to do this for him. He does it for me. *Oh, how he does it for me.*

Again, I gobble his entire shaft inside my steamy mouth and swirl my tongue up his length before clamping my lips tightly. I draw the entire length from root to tip, in and out of my silky, wet lips. Lance's fingers weave through my hair as he fucks my mouth repeatedly. His entire body shudders as thick cum fills the hollows of my cheeks. I massage his withdrawn sacs while sucking his perfect penis for every tasty drop. Lance lifts me from the ground pulling me tightly against his heaving chest. "Lisa, you and that talented mouth may actually kill me someday, but damn it I will die a happy man."

Extremely pleased by his reaction I reply, "I'm happy to know I can please my man."

"Baby, there is never any reason to doubt that. You are everything I've ever wanted or will ever want," he croons before swooning me with one of his dazzling kisses. *His kisses literally curl my toes and instantaneously make me wet.*

Turbulent Passion

Lance reaches behind me and leisurely lowers the zipper to my dress while molding me to his body. I feel my dress easing to the floor while Lance's mouth eats at mine. His hands slide under my garters to cup my cheeks and before I realize it, I am wrapped around Lance's hips and being lowered to his bed. "You could cause a man to have heart failure with those black thigh highs, garters, thong, and lace bra; baby that combo should be illegal on you. With that get up on and that talented mouth of yours, well we may never leave the room." I happily giggle as he lifts my feet over his shoulders and lowers to his knees.

"Aren't you going to remove my boots?"

"Hell no. Baby, this is a scene out of one of my fantasies," he laughs before kissing and licking the tender skin inside my thigh.

I lift my head to inquire, "I guess that means we aren't going to walk on the beach?" I receive my answer by the thrusts of Lance's tongue into my swollen, drenched opening. I quiver as he mystifies

G.L. Ross

my senses. His hands roam by thighs, stomach, and bottom. His lips wander through my cleft teasing me with puffs of breath before pulling my tender tissues between his lips and tongue.

"Do you want me to stop, for the walk on the beach?" he taunts while my juices sparkle on his lips.

"No, please don't stop," I pant and beg.

"What do you want me to do, Lisa?"

Don't ask me just do it.

"What?" I gasp, as he wickedly smiles. "Touch me, damn it, please touch me," I embarrassingly beg.

"That's what I wanted to hear," Lance playfully replies. He slides two fingers inside my greedy sex. His tongue attacks the seam of my cleft causing my back to arch from the bed. I push my sex towards his face. I feel like a kid in a toy store – *I want more, I want everything, and I want it now*. My talented *lover* unfastens my garters with one hand

Turbulent Passion

and rips my thong into with his teeth. *Did I hit the jackpot or what?* Lance increases his suction on my clit and his fingers find the ever sensitive spongy tissue that spirals me up and over the volatile edge. He jerks me to the edge of the bed as he stands and spreads my thighs. His rock hard manhood presses against my pulsating entrance. "Lisa, turn your head to the side," he commands.

"Why, I like to watch you?" I pout. *Kid in a toy store...*

"Exactly, turn your head and watch us in the mirror."

I turn my head to the left and find our profile reflected in the large mounted wall mirror. "Oh, that's cool." I watch Lance's ass cheeks tighten as his pelvis juts forward, lunging his "God's gift to me" penis deep inside my pulsing sex. Slowly he pulls and pushes his mind blowing length into my hot, sensitive opening. Both of us watch with amazement as our bodies worship and explore each other. Lance's desire begins to build along with his speed. He repositions my hips and delves deeper to find my

G.L. Ross

magical G-spot. My eyes flash wide sharing my building desire. I bite my lower lip accelerating and igniting his revving engine. Pounding into me Lance's heated gaze rakes across my bouncing breasts, "I love when your tits bounce from me fucking you senseless."

Lance angles above me rubbing his pelvis up and down my sex as he continues his frantic plunging. His fingers link with mine pinning my hands above my head. The friction between us causes a burning desire deep inside me to grow and combust. I arch against him wrapping my feet around his gorgeous, perfect ass. I push him deeper spreading the lips of my sex to handle his root. "Faster Lance, faster," I scream. His teeth scrape and bite my nipples as he delves faster and deeper inside me. "Baby, harder, deeper, please Lance," I urge.

Lance's face grimaces with strain as he masterfully controls and fights his eruption, in order to help me find mine first. Our skin pops from the sweaty suction between our bodies. Thighs flap

Turbulent Passion

against each other as our skin heats and glistens. "Oh, Lance, oh, it's happening again."

"Cum Lisa, cum. Christ baby, let go now!" I explode and squeeze Lance's cock unmercifully with my reverberating tunnel. He screams my name as he finds his well-deserved release, "Lisa, baby…you undo me," he mumbles as his face falls within my happily just fucked hair.

We spoon the rest of the evening, that is, after he removes my "come fuck me" boots. *Yes, Lance named them.* The feel of his warm body against mine is unbelievably natural and welcome. Blissfully content, we fall asleep in each other's arms, for a second night.

I wake with Lance's heartbeat pulsing against my cheek, our legs entwined, my hip pressed against one of his. His arms tenderly hold me against his rhythmic chest, as though I've always belonged there. I'm lulled by the melodic tempo of Lance's heartbeat until I feel a ticklish twitching against my thigh. I hesitantly lift the sheet to see Lance's penis

G.L. Ross

growing long and thick. *So it is true they wake with a hard-on.*

"Like what you see, baby?" he snickers before kissing my temple. Startled, I drop the sheet. "I want to make love to you, Lisa." *Didn't we just do that a few hours ago? Not that I am complaining.*

"Then by all means proceed, kind sir," I coquettishly tease.

"I want to make sure you are not too sore. I could tell you were swollen earlier." *Okay, I am officially mortified.* "Lisa, look at me." My chin tilts upwards for my eyes to absorb the beautiful man holding me. His lips softly press against mine. "Do not be embarrassed or shy with me. We share everything and that means I take care of you. Besides, I especially like caring for certain parts of you," he naughtily grins. *I love that grin.* He lightly traces and sucks my bottom lip, before sliding his tongue over mine. We explore the others' tempting tastes. My tongue searches and begs for more. *Will I ever get enough of him?* His erection now presses firmly against my hip. Lance rolls me beneath him.

Turbulent Passion

His hands plump my breasts as his lips suckle my sore nipples. His fingers find me wet and ready. Rather than his fingers rubbing against my throbbing clit, Lance slides and presses his thick, hard prowess up and down my cleft. My hips instinctively move against his. *It's really fun to masturbate with the assistance of his firmly erect penis.* Both of us moan pleasurably as we rub against each other. I grind my clit sensually against his girth as my nails dig into his ass pulling him closer. His hands and mouth devastate my breasts causing an excruciating throbbing between my legs. I want his heat inside me, now. Lance's back bows as he roughly and quickly strokes his magnificent length against my pathway. His sex grows wide and long. I feel the weight and enormity of his penis against my sex. Lance's breaths become shorter as his speed increases. My opening is generously full of wet wonder as Lance slides carefully through my tender entry. *He is extremely caring and gentle with me when required.*

Lance's devastatingly handsome face contorts as he screams my name, "Lisa! What are you doing to me?" He slows his rhythm struggling to

G.L. Ross

keep control. "You feel too good." He pulls my hands above my head and laces his fingers into my hair. His forehead lowers to rest on mine while he attempts to steady his breathing. After a few minutes of seductively burning gazes, Lance smiles at me, kisses the tip of my nose, and thrills me with four magical words I never thought I would hear from him, "I love you, Lisa." *Our hearts, minds, and bodies have truly become one.*

Turbulent Passion

Chapter Twelve

Boyfriend

This past week has been the best seven days of my life. Lisa gives the term "God-send" a new meaning. I can't believe I'm admitting this, but not seeing her the past two days has been pure hell. I never thought I would miss a woman, but I miss my Goddess.

Her trip ends today, so she will be home in Dallas tonight and has the weekend off. Unfortunately, I have to work the next two days. Of course, I have plenty to smile about, so I really shouldn't complain, now that I have her in my life *and in my bed.* Tonight I'm in San Francisco, if the weather permits. *Mother Nature is being a real bitch.* Lisa requested I call her when I made it to the hotel, no matter how late, but she may not have had three in the morning in mind when she made that request.

Tomorrow evening I'm meeting some Air Force buddies in Austin. We should have a good time on 6th and 4th streets. *Great live music in those areas.* Maybe I should invite Lisa to join us. I would like

G.L. Ross

her to meet my friends and vice versus. *Did I really say that? The guys meeting my gal? They might stroke out.* Maybe I should wait. I don't want to move too fast and frighten her away.

I am really lousy with this dating stuff. Should I send her flowers? I'll ask the guys tomorrow night how to "court" a woman. Lisa's "old fashioned" and wants a man who "courts and woos" her. *Who would have ever thought Lance Miller would be wooing a woman?*

****

Three hours late, *WTH*, I almost got the time right it's two "crack" of dawn rather than three. *I am beat and hear a sweet bed calling my name.* Fighting weather is as combative as a two hour punching bag work out. There's no way I'm calling Lisa at this hour. I'll call her in the morning, *hell it is morning.*

Thank goodness this hotel has nice, firm beds plus I lucked out with a king size bed. Can't believe I am on a PM trip and setting an alarm. *Something is majorly messed up with this picture.* I'm setting the alarm on my phone when I notice a missed

Turbulent Passion

call. How did I miss a call? "Idiot," I grunt while slamming my palm to my forehead. I still have the blasted phone on vibrate. And, of course, it's a missed call from Lisa.

Yes, I'm smiling. Only Goddess can make me smile after this day.

She left a message, "Lance, please call me. I don't care how late it is. I need to hear your voice. Miss you." Baby sounds upset and I don't think it's because she misses me.

After four rings Lisa sleepily answers my call, "Hello."

Softly I reply, "Hey baby. You said to call no matter what time."

"I know and I'm glad you called. Was the weather bad?" She's beginning to sound a bit more coherent.

"Honey, if you are sleeping we can talk later this morning."

G.L. Ross

"It is morning, isn't it? No, I'm awake and I need to hear your voice, so tell me about your day, please." She yawns, drops, and quickly retrieves the phone all in a split second.

"Lisa, you sound upset. What's going on?"

"Lance, I'm already feeling better. I knew talking to you would make everything okay. Tell me about the storms. Is the weather bad in San Francisco?"

Now I'm getting pissed - she won't answer my damn question. "Lisa, enough. What is wrong and don't change the subject to the weather and my day. Answer me," I bark.

The line goes silent and then I hear her sniffle. Shit! I've made her cry. Lance you asshole. You are a lousy boyfriend.

"I'm sorry I asked you to call. I know you're tired. Go to sleep. We can talk after we both get some rest."

Time for a new approach, Lance. "Don't hang up. I love you, Lisa. Never apologize for

Turbulent Passion

needing me, in any way, shape, or form. Obviously something or someone has upset you. It's my job to take care of you, so what's wrong and don't say 'nothing'?"

Lisa sniffs several times while choking back her tears, *which I probably have caused, damn it,* before answering my question in almost a whimper, "Wayne, Wayne is what's wrong."

That must have been the fucker in her room in Austin. My blood begins to boil.

"Continue," I abruptly order.

"Please don't be upset with me, Lance."

"Upset with you? Why would I be upset with you?" She has to get over this fear of me hurting her or being upset with her.

"I finally returned his calls and text messages. I knew…" I halt her mid-sentence.

"Excuse me? He has been contacting you repetitively and you didn't tell me? Now that upsets me, Lisa."

G.L. Ross

"This is why I didn't tell you. You're upset."
I hear the tears and sniffles growing once again. *Shit.*

"Lisa, I'm not upset - with you. Continue the
story, please."

She stutters through sniffles and choked
back tears, "Pro-mise me you won't say an-y-thing
un-til I fin-ish, o-kay?"

"I promise, baby. Tell me what happened."

"I called him to ex-plain I wouldn't be visiting him in Austin and that we were o-ver. I
explained I was in a seri-ous relationship and hoped
we could con-tinue to be friends. He called me a
tease and said no man would want me as in-
experienced as I am." *I may kill this fucker.* "I told
him I was sorry he was upset and that you and I had
been da-ting at the same time I was seeing him. He
called me all kinds of horrible names." *This asshole
has my Goddess crying and feeling inadequate. He
and I will have our day.* "I'm sorry I'm cry-ing and
so emo-tional."

Turbulent Passion

"Baby, don't apologize for anything. This guy is an ass and doesn't deserve to even look your way. I will handle him."

"No, Lance! This is why I wasn't going to tell you. Just let him go. All I ever need is to hear you say you love and miss me. That makes everything okay." *She has no idea what she does to me.*

"Lisa, I am here to care for you, which means no one will disrespect you."

"But, Lance…"

"Enough!" Damn it, Lance…

"I'm sorry I yelled. Please baby, no more tears. I can't handle you crying when I can't hold you. I do love you and I do miss you. *Man do I miss you.* It's killing me you're upset and we aren't together. No one should ever upset my beautiful Goddess. I'll handle this and I don't want to hear another word about this lowlife. Now, baby, take a deep breath, calm down, and tell me about the rest of your day."

G.L. Ross

Lisa followed my directions and after forty minutes she hung up only because she could barely keep her eyes open. Twice she started breathing deeply due to dozing, even though she denied it both times. I, on the other hand, cannot sleep. That, Wayne fucker, lives in Austin; I think my Air Force buddies and I may have to visit Mr. Brighton - *somewhere away from work.*

Baby Girl

I can't believe Wayne called me those horrible names. I understand him being hurt, but his reaction was downright hateful. We only went out twice and we never claimed to be exclusive. I'm sure he was seeing other women. So, why be cruel? *Perhaps Wayne has never been turned down?*

No matter what his reaction was extremely hurtful. I hope I never see him again. Regrettably the odds are I will run into him when I travel through Austin, but he won't make a scene at work - *thank goodness.*

Turbulent Passion

I miss Lance. I wish he were coming home tonight. He was incredibly sweet and caring, this morning, in between orders and commands. *I did ask him to call and I knew he would be exhausted, so I can't complain about his attitude. Besides, Lance is a control freak.* Also, men don't like emotional women, *especially crybabies*, and I was both when we spoke.

It's too bad I'm not on Lance's trip. I would love to meet his buddies and create a new, happy memory for Austin overnights.

I wonder...should I? Okay, if there is a two day trip in give away, with an Austin overnight this evening, then I was meant to work that trip and see Lance. If there isn't a trip then I am supposed to stay home and *do laundry.* What fun. *Please let there be a trip.*

Hot damn! Not only is there an Austin two day there is one with my friend, Nick. *Lisa, get packing, you have a party to attend.*

Nick and I are visiting during ground time in Kansas City when I decide to question him regarding

G.L. Ross

whether or not I should crash Lance's Air Force reunion. "So Nick, in your opinion should I call Lance and let him know I will be there tonight or should I surprise him?"

"Lisa, let's plan on going to 6th street with our crew. Once we get to the hotel you can see if Lance has signed in and if so, once we get to a club, text and invite him to stop by and say hello, with his buddies. But, if we get there first, leave a note for him at the front desk letting him know you picked up a trip, and are here, and on your way to 6th street."

I contemplate Nick's idea. "That's a good plan, Nick. We will see what happens when we make it to Austin. I sincerely hope he is happy to see me or else you may be playing nurse mate to me tonight."

"I can hold back your hair with the best baby girl. But, I have a feeling someone else's fingers will be in your hair tonight."

"Nick," I holler and giggle. *Inwardly I hope he is right.* I desperately want Lance's fingers in my hair *and many other places.*

Turbulent Passion

The Crowne Plaza lobby is an architectural work of art. The crystal chandeliers and oriental rugs add extravagance in its loveliest form. "Lisa, what is Lance's inbound flight number?" Nick asks while signing in at the front desk.

"1533, I think. Is there a flight number similar to that on the Pilot sign in sheet?"

"How about 3315? Are you dyslexic Lisa?" Nick jabs.

"No, but I am blond," I sass. Nick is such a doll. I need to find him a good gal. "So, what's the verdict are they here?"

"Nope, not yet. Here's your key, my dear."

"Is Angie going to sign in later this evening or just meet us at the airport tomorrow?" Our third FA lives in Austin, so she is going home to her real bed. Often flight crew members who are in their home city will still come back to the hotel, at some point, so they are present for lobby. But, some choose to meet at the airport the following day. Depending on the size of our aircraft and destination we may

G.L. Ross

have a fourth, fifth, or even sixth flight attendant join us.

"She will meet us at the airport. Let's change clothes and head over to 6th street. Trace and Melissa, my friends from Canada, are already there. The guys mentioned they are changing clothes and heading that way, too."

"Sounds like a fun group, knock on my door when you're ready. I'll check the front desk, on our way out, to see if Lance has arrived, if not I'll leave him a note."

I sure am glad Nick is on this trip with me. No matter what we will have a good time.

I checked the front desk and Lance hasn't arrived so I left a note as Nick suggested. The person at the counter said Lance's crew was on the van and heading this way. He guessed they were about ten minutes out, so I have no doubt I will hear from Lance in a bit - in either a good or bad way. *Please be good. Please be happy I am here.*

While exiting the hotel Nick chimes in, "So baby girl what did you put in the note?" I find it

Turbulent Passion

humorous Nicky calls me "baby girl" since I am older than him.

"Don't laugh, but I mentioned if he wanted a roommate for the evening to give me a ring. Is that too forward or corny?" Lance is a ladies' man whereas I am a total novice when it comes to this relationship/sex thing, for lack of a better word, so I need a lot of guidance. "I don't know how to be a seductress, Nick."

Nick pulls me in for a sideways hug as we continue to follow the lopsided sidewalk to 6th Street. "Lisa, you are a seductress without trying, which is why you are the only woman to ever land Lance Miller. Baby, trust me, you're definitely not being too forward and I guarantee 'corny' is not the word that will come to Lance's mind when he reads your note."

"You're sure?" I ask a second time.

Nick croons, "Baby girl, you have him eating out of the palm of your hand." My adorable friend places a kiss on my right palm, before threading his fingers with mine. "Now hold on to my hand while I weave us through this crowd."

G.L. Ross

I clasp Nick's hand tightly as we bump and squeeze through groups and individuals standing in the cramped, busy street. The sounds of Jazz and CW music waft and filter into the concrete passageway. "I recognize that CW bar. I've been there and they have great music and cheap beer," I yell to Nick over the music and street chatter. He nods and pulls me towards the packed club. Before entering I squeeze his hand to gain his attention. "My phone vibrated. Let me check it. Why don't you text your Canadian friends and let them know where we are."

"Sounds good," he mouths. The music is incredibly loud. Fortunately the song is about to end, so maybe Nick and I can communicate without screaming or lip reading. *I wonder if I will have any hearing, by the end of the evening.*

"Is it Lance?" Nick inquires. He receives his answer when he sees my bright and shiny smile.

"He is on his way." *My smile is from ear to ear.* I am a happy girl.

Turbulent Passion

"So, I take it he is happy and 'up' for a roomie tonight?" Nick says with inflection on the "up."

"Yes," I blush and giggle. "Did you reach your friends?"

"Yep, they're on their way. They said they would pay their tab and head over here. Let's get you a glass of wine and me a beer."

"You know me so well, Nicky." Once again Nick laces his fingers with mine, then places a kiss on my cheek, and routes us through the tables to the bar. Somehow Nick gets the bartender to comprehend our order. *Bartenders must be gifted lip readers.* Nicks friends join us and I recognize the guy, Trace, from an overnight. More than likely from one of our Sacramento, Cancun, or San Diego overnights, where there are bunches of crews in the bar.

Nick and I down our first round and make our way to the dance floor. Nick is a marvelous dancer. All the ladies are eyeing him and wishing they were me. *Eat your heart out, ladies.* The song is almost over when I feel a large pair of hands on my waist. I smile, assuming they are Lance's hands, until Nick jerks me towards his chest. "Get your hands off my girl," Nick snarls. I turn to face my groper and am dumbstruck, *it's Wayne.*

"Hey Lisa, may I have this dance?" he congenially asks, *as though he never called me a cunt.*

"Wayne, what are you doing here and why would you want to have anything to do with me?"

"Lisa, you don't have to talk to this guy," Nick says while wrapping his arm around my waist and pulling me close to his side.

"It's okay Nick. I can handle this. Let me deal with Wayne." He looks at me questionably, but I squeeze his hand and mouth "one song." He nods his understanding of my message and heads towards the bar. "Okay Wayne, one dance."

"Thanks Lisa. So, is that the guy that took my place?" Wayne's voice is tight and edgy. He's obviously still angry. I smell the whiskey on his breath. His hand around my waist tightens and tugs

Turbulent Passion

me closer. I keep leaning and pushing back, but he continues to win our battle of strength.

I do my best to stay calm, while still trying to place distance between our bodies. "His name is Nick, he is not the one, and no one took your place. You were a friend and can still be one, if you so choose." Wayne jerks me back against his body and rakes me with an angry sneer. I tense and the hairs on the back of my neck prickle. I push against his chest to distance myself. *This dance is over as far as I am concerned.* Wayne grips my left bicep and yanks me out of the club onto the street. "Wayne, what do you think you are doing?" His eyes are cold as he continues to pull me farther away from Nick and the club. The street is too loud and crowded for anyone around us to realize I am being taken against my will. I hear the song ending in the distance and pray Nick will come looking for me, *soon.*

Wayne hauls me between two buildings and behind a trash dumpster. I try to break his grip, but to no avail. "Wayne let me go. You are hurting me." Our voices echo in the drab, dirty, empty alley. I pray

G.L. Ross

someone will walk this way soon to fool around and hear my cry for help.

My assailant backs me against the brick wall and barricades me with a hand on each side of my shoulders. His body leans and presses completely against mine. His face enshrouds itself with my hair and the curve of my neck. Wayne's breath settles heavily against my ear. "Did you give him what was mine to take, Lisa?" *Oh God, please get me out of here.*

He pins my thighs with his and takes both of my wrists above my head trapped in his one large hand. His free hand snakes its way under my skirt to my panties. *Please Lord, don't let this happen.* "This is mine," he sneers engaging his eyes with mine while his fingers delve through my cleft.

"Wayne let me go. You don't want me like this," I plead.

Fueled by anger Wayne rips my panties and pushes his hard on against my tense sex. "I will have you any way I damn well please," he grunts while shoving two fingers inside me. The pain rips through

Turbulent Passion

me. I am dry and frightened. I push my hips back into the wall trying to prevent his passage. He removes his fingers but only to unbutton and unzip his jeans.

"Wayne, please," I beg through tears.

"I would have been gentle for your first time if you had been mine. But, this is what you get for being a damn tease." His free hand drags my skirt above my waist. His mouth attacks my lips, bruising and biting them. I taste the whiskey remnants on his lips. "Open your damn mouth, Lisa," he orders. I fight to turn my face, but I'm distracted and reeling from the feel of his pulsing sex approaching my opening. "You damn cunt, open your mouth and legs for me," he angrily howls.

I scream for help, "Someone help me. He is hurting…" His mouth slams against mine to silence me. My head bounces off the bricks. Black spots erupt before my eyes. He is relentless as he pushes his erection between my thighs trying to find my opening. I feel his pre-cum on the inside of my thigh. I struggle to twist my torso or legs, anything to stop him. He attempts to push his tongue into my mouth, but I bite his tongue as hard as physically possible.

G.L. Ross

"You bitch!" he screams and slaps me, "If you want it rough then I will give it to you rough." I taste my own blood on my lips as he backhands me repeatedly.

His pelvis slams by body against the hard, immobile wall. My head reels. I swear I hear my name, "Lisa! Lisa, where are you?" Am I hallucinating? It sounds as though my name is being sung in a round. *Answer them Lisa!*

"Help," I whimper. My head and back ache from being rammed against the mortar.

"Shut up you cunt," he grunts while ripping my shirt apart. His teeth wound my breasts and nipples.

I dig deep inside my soul and find the strength to scream while my mouth is free, "I'm here, help!"

"Lance, this way," I hear Nick yell.

"Get off of her you fucker," I hear Lance howl as he jerks Wayne from me. I collapse into Nick's arms as Lance pulverizes Wayne's face.

Turbulent Passion

"Lance, don't," I whimper. Nick pulls my face against his chest preventing me from watching the bloodbath.

"Don't you ever touch her again or even look at her," Lance rages between punches.

I hear Lance's buddies imploring him to stop. *Please make him stop.* "That's him. He was attacking Lance's girl." I turn to the voice I don't recognize and see police officers pulling Lance off of Wayne. Lance's fists are bloody and ripped. He is covered in sweat and Wayne's blood from head to toe. His buddies hold him back as the police pull Wayne to his feet.

Lance snarls, "Get your fuckin' dick back in your pants before I rip it from your body."

"You? You are the one banging the virgin? The manwhore and the virgin, fucking perfect," Wayne sarcastically spews as the police cuff him.

"Get him out of here before I kill him," Lance says between gritted teeth.

G.L. Ross

"Lance shut up," one of his Air Force friends warns. "Go take care of your girl."

Lance turns towards my trembling tears and his anger transforms to compassion and fear. "Baby," he cries as Nick rotates me into Lance's protective arms. His heart races against my cheek as his hands stroke the length of my hair. "You're safe, baby. You're safe. I have you, Lisa. I'm here. I will take care of you. I promise."

Turbulent Passion

Chapter Thirteen

Mine

"Alright guys, I'm finally here so let's get this party started," I laugh while slapping backs and shaking hands with my buds.

William responds, "Hey man we're glad you're finally here, better late than never, but now let's hurry and grab some beers."

Tom continues William's train of thought, "… and find some Southern women."

"Speaking of fine, Southern women…" I decide to throw the information out and endure the ramifications. It will be worth the guy's harassment to see and be with Lisa.

Ken interjects, "Hell no, say it isn't so. Has a woman really lassoed Lance Miller?"

I smile and they all begin to bombard me with one liners and questions. "I need to meet this woman. She must be something to pussy whip you, Lance," Randall responds in jest.

G.L. Ross

"Where did you meet her?" Tom interjects.

"If you'll hang on a minute I'll fill you in and by the way it's your lucky day – you get to meet the Goddess," I enthusiastically and proudly reply. Only Miss Price could turn me from a manwhore to a man who woos and courts a woman, *and is open and proud about it!*

Harry jumps in, "The Goddess?"

The guys tease and laugh until I interrupt, "We will see who is laughing when you meet her."

A chorus of "whoa" and "go get her man" erupts from the guys.

"Let's grab a shot of whiskey and then we'll all grab a piece of ass." Everyone erupts in laughter. "But Lisa is mine." I interject as the shots arrive, "And leave it to Harry to have the shots already ordered."

After another round of shots we head to the CW bar where Lisa texted she, Nick, and some other International Air folks are dancing and drinking. I can't wait to wrap my arms around my sassy, sexy

Turbulent Passion

lady love. *Lisa gets really frisky when she indulges herself with wine.* I plan on making sure she has as much fun, if not more, than the fun I plan on enjoying tonight *and in the morning.*

I'm glad I decided to wait to invite her. The fact she took a chance to come see me and picked up a trip to possibly be with me is a great gift. It's the best gift a woman has ever given me. *She missed me.*

I really am excited for her to meet my friends. My buds are gifted, upstanding men. They represent the disciplined, respectful side of me, along with the wild and crazy guy facet. I know they are gonna love her. I, of course, am *in love* with her, *which scares the hell out of me.* I can't believe I just admitted that and didn't break into a cold sweat. *You're maturing, man. There may be hope for you.*

Chris Young's hit song, "Aw Naw," is bursting through the door of the bar as my flyboys, *that's what Lisa would call them,* and I arrive. I sent a text to let her know we were on our way, but I don't see her anywhere. I thought she might be waiting by the door. *No, I'm not pouting.* She's probably in the

G.L. Ross

ladies room primping. *Isn't that what ladies do in there?*

"Where is this Goddess, Lance," Tom teasingly asks.

"I'm looking. She's here." *Where is she?*

"Lance!" I hear my name over the roar. My eyes search the crowd and finally land upon Nick's waving arms, high in the air.

"Hey guys this way," I direct.

"Back up Lance," Nick yells. "We have a problem. Let's go outside."

Cold chills race up and down my back. A sick feeling punches me in the gut. Lisa is in trouble, *I know it*. I feel it in my soul. We step into the street, which isn't much quieter than the club. The guys are all asking what's going on and my heart is racing. I grab Nick as soon as we are on the noisy, crowded street. "What is going on Nick? Where the hell is Lisa?"

Turbulent Passion

Nick's face is flustered. His voice is frustrated and nervous as he explains, "We were dancing; a guy comes up, interrupts us, and asks to dance with Lisa." *Already not a fan of this story.* "I didn't like the guy. He gave off a bad vibe."

I interrupt, "Then why the hell did you let her dance with him?"

"Lance, I told her not to, but she said she could handle him for one dance. She knew him."

"Then what's the problem? Where is she?" The feeling in my gut is now raw fear.

The guys have sensed the fact something is wrong and has to do with Lisa. The protect and defend character in all of us Armed Forces guys has risen to the top. Each one of them has crowded in to hear the discussion between Nick and me. "Where is she Nick?" I scream.

"I don't know." *My fists clench at my sides.* Nick hurriedly continues his explanation, "I came back to retrieve her when the song ended and they were gone. She won't answer her cell. I'm really

G.L. Ross

worried. I was heading out to look for her when I saw you."

"Shit!" I rapidly interrogate Nick, "Why did you not watch her the entire time? Who was he? Did you know him? Did she say his name?" Fear fills my veins. My blood turns cold. *Don't take her from me God. Not now!*

"She said his name. It was…" *Hell Nick, any day now!*

With both hands full of his shirt I scream, "What the hell was it Nick?"

Nick nervously twitches. "Dwayne? No, it started with a W."

Before he can answer I grunt, "Wayne." *The fucker.* I rip out my phone and show the guys Lisa's picture. "Half of you take that side and split both ways. The rest take this side with us. Look down the side streets and alleys. Listen for screams, if possible, over all this cacophony. Find her, please," I beg.

I run from building to building, searching the side streets. I check periodically the other side

Turbulent Passion

and behind me for signals from my guys, that hopefully, they have found her…*and she is safe.* Nick and I create a system where one stops to check a side street while the other runs ahead to the next building. We continue passing each other searching and listening for the dreaded scream, *which my gut tells me is unfortunately coming.*

Panic creeps from my feet through my limbs. In my mind I dismiss it and follow my training. I will find her. We will find her *and I will kill the fucker.* I promised to protect her. Why didn't she wait at the hotel for me? She knew he lived here.

I turn back and the guys on my side, who went the opposite way, signal they are returning. Nick runs ahead of me as I check the team on the opposite side.

I motion I'm going forward. Adrenaline has taken over as I reach accelerated speeds I've never achieved. I'm about to pass Nick when I hear him yell, "Lance, this way!"

My legs dart me past Nick. Bile fills my throat as I see Wayne attacking Lisa. "Get off of her you fucker," I scream as I hurl him to the pavement. My fists repeatedly pound into his face and sides. My knees pin his arms as I beat his head against the street. "You piece of trash. You touched my Goddess and you will pay," I erupt. Through the mist I hear Lisa's cries, but all I can interpret are the screams from Lisa when I approached her and this lowlife was ripping her clothes and hurting her, *perhaps raping her. Please God, no.* The thought of him raping her releases an uncontrollable rage inside me, which had been lying dormant, until now. I'm still throwing punches when my guys pull me unwillingly from the asshole, lowlife, piece of shit, fucker.

Police officers pull Wayne to his feet and I am ready to "Lorena Bobbitt" his dick when I see it hanging freely from his lowered jeans. I scream for him to put it away before I rip it from his body and kill his ass. One of my guys turns me to face Lisa and my heart sinks. Nick is holding my bruised, crying baby. The piece of shit has beaten and bloodied her. Her clothes are ripped. Her flesh exposed. My eyes fill with tears as I wrap the love of my life securely in my arms. *Thank God she is alive.*

Turbulent Passion

I console us both with my promises. Time after time I promise to take care of her. I promise to keep her safe. I stroke her hair as she soaks my shirt with her blood and tears. A police officer leads us to an ambulance at the end of the side street. Lisa clings to me as we climb inside the ambulance. The paramedic injects her with a medication to calm her as I cradle her in my arms. I wish they could totally sedate her, but I'm sure she has a concussion. The sirens blare as we rapidly make our way to the hospital. My mind races with the practicalities of what needs to be done. Nick promised to call their Scheduling Department, so they are aware of Lisa's situation and need for replacement. I will contact Pilot Scheduling once Lisa is settled. *There is no way I'm leaving her side.* In spite of the blood, I nuzzle Lisa's hair and kiss her temple. My thoughts are interrupted by the paramedic, "Mam, I hate to upset you but I need to swab some of your injuries for DNA, so I may then clean and bandage them." Lisa turns her face to him, but doesn't utter a word.

"Mam, we are about to arrive at the hospital. You will require stitches and the doctors will want to know if you were raped." Lisa remains silent. "Mam,

G.L. Ross

I know this is upsetting, but we need to know all the facts, so we can give you the best possible care." Still no response. *Please, say he didn't rape you, baby. Please say I got to you in time.*

"Baby, look at me." Lisa turns her face to mine. Our eyes lock. My voice shakes as I ask, "Lisa, did Wayne rape you?" My heart skips a beat as her vacant eyes fill with tears. Bile reaches my mouth. I swallow hard. I must remain strong, for Lisa. "Lisa, please tell me," I whisper. "I love you no matter what. You know that, don't you?" My eyes swim in tears as the ambulance abruptly stops. The doors fly open as attendants stand waiting with a gurney. I continue to cradle Goddess in my arms as I step from the ambulance. "I'm carrying her. Lead the way," I order the hospital orderlies.

We are lead to a room with blue curtains separating the individual areas. The white sheets and sterile area are depressing and frightening even to me. Lisa's arms cling to me, while her face buries itself against the slope of my neck. The feel of her shaky breath and tears against my skin should be

Turbulent Passion

depressing, but I am beyond thankful she is alive. *She is alive. Thank you, Lord.*

A female doctor enters the room and request I place Lisa on the metal bed, with the ultra-thin mattress. Lisa shakes her head negatively and begins to sob. I lower her to the bed, sit beside her, and keep one arm wrapped behind her neck and shoulders. I search the doctor's eyes for approval. She nods okay, but I can tell it's a temporary agreement.

"Lisa, my name is Nancy O'Malley and I am the doctor assigned to your case. Do you understand me?"

Lisa nods affirmatively.

"Lisa, I know this is difficult, but I need to ask you some questions." Lisa's eyes close briefly. She inhales a slow, deep breath. I can tell she is preparing herself, for the inevitable. "Lisa, were you raped?" Again, the deafening silence permeates the room. "Lisa, nod your head yes or no."

Lisa inhales deeply again before speaking. "I need water," she roughly ekes from her mouth. I jump for a glass of water. The nurse enters our area

G.L. Ross

delivering a pitcher of ice water and a plastic wrapped cup. I urgently return to Lisa's side with a full cup of water. The nurse and I assist in sitting her up. I hold the cup to the edge of Lisa's bleeding mouth. She cringes as the water stings her abused lips, but is appreciative of the cold water passing through her mouth and throat, "Thank you."

The doctor tries again, "Lisa, you need stitches, along with x-rays and other tests. I cannot start those procedures until I know if we need a rape kit."

"He tried." *My body tenses as my heart drops.* "I felt his semen on my thighs," she chokes. *I should have killed him.* "He pushed against my opening, but I don't think he ever entered me, with his penis." She shivers. Tears flow down her beaten cheeks. I see the impression of his ring on her right cheek. *Damn him.*

"Did something else enter your vagina, Lisa," the doctor investigates.

Turbulent Passion

Lisa sips more water before whispering, "His fingers." My jaw clenches. "I'm so sorry Lance," she cries.

"Lisa, baby." I pull her against my heart. "This is not your fault and you do not need to apologize to anyone, especially me." I cradle and rock her while stroking her nape. *God I love this woman. I literally hurt for her.*

"Since there is a chance semen may have entered you and there could be vaginal tears, I will need to do a vaginal exam and rape kit. Do I have your approval, Lisa?"

"Yes," she speaks and nods. The nurse re-enters the room and hands the doctor a cup containing a single pill.

"Lisa, this is a 'morning after' pill." Lisa's frightened eyes shoot to mine.

I kiss her temple before softly answering her unspoken question, "It's okay baby, take the pill."

The doctor continues with her explanation, "Lisa, I am merely being proactive. The odds are

G.L. Ross

semen was not implanted and you will not become pregnant, but I would like for you to be protected. It is your decision." Lisa reaches for the cup holding the pill. I hold the water as her trembling hand places the pill inside her mouth. She sips the water and swallows the pill to remove any chance of being impregnated, *with Satan's offspring.*

"Sir, I will need you to step out of the room while I examine Miss Price."

I stand to leave, but Lisa grips my arm. "Baby, I will be back. I am not leaving. These ladies will take good care of you." I smile appreciatively at the nurse and doctor. "I am sure Nick and the guys are in the waiting room, by now. Let me tell them you will be okay, alright?"

"Okay," she answers regretfully.

"Lisa, after we finish the vaginal exam we will need to have x-rays taken of your chest, back, and head. So, sir, take your time. We will be busy for about forty-five minutes."

I lower my lips to gently brush against Lisa's bruised and swelling lips and cheeks, before

Turbulent Passion

whispering in her ear, "I love you. You are safe. I promise." Our eyes engage and I finally recognize trust in her eyes, *for me, for us.*

His

As I settle into the hospital bed in my private room the doctor informs me of my condition, "Lisa, we are keeping you overnight due to your concussion. The radiologist will read your films in the morning. If everything is clear we will release you. I did find some lacerations and tears in your vaginal area. The nurse will come in shortly with an antibiotic suppository to be inserted vaginally. An oral antibiotic has also been prescribed to prevent any sexually transmitted diseases. You will be contacted within 24-48 hours with your lab results. I will also give you two prescriptions to have filled when you are released. The nurse will be waking you every three hours throughout your stay due to your concussion. I've requested an anxiety medication for you tonight. Do you have any questions for me?"

What? Entirely too much information when my head is throbbing. "Where's Lance?"

G.L. Ross

"He will be here shortly. We haven't shared your room assignment with him, yet. I want you settled, before you have any visitors." A middle-aged, Asian nurse enters the room with my medications. "I will leave you in Peggy's capable hands. I'll be back tomorrow to examine you and hopefully release you." She clasps my hand between hers; the sincerity in her eyes warms me. "Lisa, you are going to be okay. He did not penetrate you vaginally with his penis. The penetration was with his fingers, only. I did not find semen inside your vagina when I swabbed and examined you. Lisa, your wounds will heal externally and internally, but you may want to seek psychological counseling for your mental wounds. I would like to send a psychiatrist to consult with you tomorrow."

"No," I abruptly answer.

"Lisa, counseling is nothing to be ashamed of, in fact, it usually helps."

"I am a licensed counselor. If I feel I need counseling I promise I will seek help."

Turbulent Passion

"Very well, Peggy will assist you with your medications. I hope you are able to rest peacefully." *Rest peacefully? You are waking me every three hours.*

Peggy is a very nice person, but this vaginal suppository/cream thing is gross. I want a shower. I want Wayne off of me. *I want Lance.* "Peggy, may I take a shower, please?" I plead.

"Lisa, we just administered the medication. I will come back in an hour and if you are up to it I will assist you in showering then. Okay?"

"Okay, I guess." At least I am out of those clothes.

"Here is Motrin for your pain and an Ativan for your anxiety. I will be back in a bit for your vitals. The control for the bed is here on the side. This control is for the television and if your need to page me. Would you like for me to turn on the television?"

"No thank-you. I'm going to try and rest until Lance gets here." I roll to my side searching for a comfortable position, but every inch of my body

G.L. Ross

screams. I observe my surroundings and the room is nice. I think it is nicer than my apartment. *Everything is larger and nicer than my apartment.* The oak hardwood floors complement the tan leather recliner. The view out the window is full of sparkling lights from the Austin skyline. Maybe tomorrow I will feel like sitting on the window seat. The medicine relaxes me, as I begin to fade I wonder once again - *Where is Lance?*

Masculine voices reverberate in the distance. Am I dreaming? Is it Wayne? No… "No! Leave me alone," I scream.

I thrash the sheets as hands grasp my biceps. "Lisa, wake up. Wake up, baby."

"Should I call the nurse, Lance?"

"No Nick. She'll hear my voice and wake. Lisa, open your eyes. It's Lance and Nick. Open. Your. Eyes."

Instinctively I respond to Lance's commanding voice. My lashes flutter open. My eyes slowly focus in the dim light to view Lance's beautiful facial features. *He is here.*

Turbulent Passion

"That's my girl," he croons while stroking my cheek with his knuckle.

Nick inquires, "Bad dream, baby girl?" I turn my head and find Nick's concerned chocolate brown eyes filling with tears.

Placing my hand over his I do my best to convince him, "I'm okay Nicky. I will be fine. No tears. You hear me?" Nick wipes his tears with the back of his hand and attempts a smile.

"Yes, mam, I brought your stuff over from the hotel." Lance slides in beside me shifting me where I'm able to recline in his arms and on his chest. Nick continues, "I called Scheduling and you have been pulled from your trips tomorrow and Monday. I gave the doctor the FMLA paperwork to complete. I didn't call your parents. I wasn't sure if you would want me to; should I call them?"

I motion for Nick to lean near me. I kiss his cheek and squeeze his hand appreciatively. "Thank you for doing all of that for me. No, don't call my parents. I will explain everything to them when I get

G.L. Ross

home. They'll need to see I'm really okay. I can't thank you enough, Nick."

Tears tumble from his eyes. Through a choked voice Nick justifies his tears, "It's my fault you are here. I never should have left you with him. I'm really sorry Lisa. I'm so sorry." His face falls against my thigh as he sobs uncontrollably.

Tears streak my cheeks as I stroke Nick's hair with my fingertips. "Nick, it is not your fault." My words become terse as I allow anger to bubble and surface, "He caused this. You and I did nothing wrong. A person should be safe when on a public dance floor. If this is your fault then it is mine, also."

Lance expeditiously admonishes me, "This is not your fault."

"Exactly," I respond and continue, "And it is not Nick's fault either. Now, no more tears. I love you Nick and I appreciate you and Lance finding and saving me – more than you will ever know. I wasn't raped, at least not in the way you are thinking." I shake my head and squeeze Nick's hand. "Go to the

Turbulent Passion

hotel, get some rest. Did they pull you from the trip, also?"

"Yea, they did."

"Good, go get some sleep. I am going to try and rest, too. I love you."

"I love you, baby girl. Lance, call me if I can do anything."

"I will." Lance stands and shakes his hand. Nick kisses my forehead then solemnly exits the room.

Lance returns to the bed protectively holding me, guarding me. I sigh and place my cheek against the rise and fall of his strong, rippled chest. He dims the lights and curls his body around mine. Not a single word is spoken. Lance's eyes caress my injured heart and soul. His fingers brush my hair from my face and I swear this very moment is the most intimate moment we have shared. I relax knowing I am completely safe and protected in *my* astounding man's arms. My lashes flutter to stay open, but the medicine is strong willed. I feel Lance's

G.L. Ross

soft lips against my forehead as I fall into a deep, hopefully dreamless, sleep.

Two and a half hours later Peggy enters the room to wake me and takes my vitals. "Lisa, he should be in the recliner not on this bed with you. You can't be comfortable," she admonishes.

I whisper my reply being careful not to wake him, "I honestly am able to sleep because he is holding me. Please?"

"Fine. Your blood pressure and temperature are normal. If you would like to shower you may."

"Thank you. I will in a little while," I appreciatively smile.

"Call me when you are ready."

"Yes mam," I respond.

I curl back against Lance. His arm pulls me closer before he brushes his lips sweetly across mine. "I will help you shower, baby." I behold and enjoy my sweet man's smile.

Turbulent Passion

"I was planning on you showering with me,
but I didn't want Peggy to know. Do you mind if we
do it now? I want him off of me." Tears begin to
flood my eyes, but I fight them back. Lance loses his
smile, but remains my rock. His muscular arms lift,
cradle, and carry me into the shower area. Lance
undresses first. His sculpted body still affects and
astounds me. You would think I would be fearful of a
man's body and touch, but I am completely
comforted by Lance. *I do trust him.*

Ever so gently Lance unties my hospital
gown and slips it from my battered body. My
strength begins to collapse as Lance's eyes view my
multiple abrasions and bruises. The temperature of
the water is masterfully adjusted by my Prince
Charming. He steps in first, with his back shielding
the force of the water from me. His fingers lace with
mine and encourage me to join him. I step in and face
his broad chest. With a tender touch, Lance turns my
body and begins to lather my back with the liquid
soap. Initially the soap stings my abrasions, but
Lance quickly responds with a soft washcloth rinsing
warm water across my back. My gentle giant
stimulates my damaged nerve endings as he

G.L. Ross

endearingly shampoos and conditions my hair. My head aches, but his strokes are tender and loving. While the conditioner remains in my hair, Lance bathes the curve of my bottom and legs. His hands lead my hips to turn and face him. He continues carefully stroking and washing my body, until he reaches my sex. His body tenses. His head lowers. I slide my fingers through his wet wavy locks. The release of his held breath overwhelms me. If possible, my man aches as much as I do. His head tips to look at me as he remains on his knees. The warm water rushes over me washing away the grime of my past – *yes, my past. On his knees, in front of me, is my future.*

"Lance, wash him away. Wash him away from every inch of me. Replace his anger filled touches with your loving ones. Touch what is yours and only yours, please."

We both tense as Lance applies the soap to his fingers. I want to feel his skin touching my skin. He begins the cathartic cleansing by slowly, stroking my inner thighs. I close my eyes, breathing deeply. Lance places a kiss against my tender skin. I force

Turbulent Passion

myself to open my eyes. Gently, he rinses the soap away. More soap is applied against the top of my sex. Lance checks my eyes for continued approval. Our eyes stay locked as his soapy fingers slide through my tortured cleft. I hiss as the soap hits my lacerations. Lance freezes his movements. His pain filled eyes remain locked with mine as I whisper, "Continue, please." His soapy fingers slide across and around every part of my vaginal area. Lance grasps the shower handle and lowers the warm stream of water to my sex. In the most intimate of ways, he washes all of the filth and grime from me. I watch my ugly, vicious past disappear through the drain as tears trickle down my punished cheeks. My future stands and sweetly washes the conditioner from my hair, before showering his body in front of me.

As he begins to wash his sex my trembling hands replace his. "I need to do this, for us. No fear. I trust you and need a new vision for my mind. I need to remove this obstacle standing between us. This ugliness, this fear needs to be obliterated now." Lance responds by removing his hand and pouring soap onto my palm. I slowly lather soap along his

G.L. Ross

length and between his legs. Lance hisses between his teeth. I know he is fighting his masculine urges. He leans his head back against the shower wall, but he can't control the lengthening of his gorgeous erection. His penis brings pleasure, not pain. *Imprint that on your brain, Lisa.* My body aches for his sweet touch, but my mind knows it cannot happen - for me - now.

I continue stroking his widening girth. "Lisa, don't." His hands capture mine.

"I want to. Let me. I need to know you still find me desirable." Tears stream down my cheeks.

My sweet, sweet man weaves his fingers through my hair. "I do desire you, always. That hasn't changed and never will."

"Then let me do this. Let me make you cum." Insistence resounds from my eyes.

Lance steps back pressing the length of his body against the shower wall. My soapy fingers grip and stroke the length of his pulsing desire, *for me.* The heavily ribbed veins throb throughout his length as he finally allows his desire to grow. His moans

Turbulent Passion

excite me and allow me to focus on his pleasure rather than my pain. His hips begin to push against my strokes. "Faster, baby. Grip me tighter." When I see he is about to cum I slide his penis between the skin of my thighs. "Lisa, no."

"Not into me. Slide between my thighs so I may feel you." Lance understands and places his throbbing, heated rod between the intimate space of my thighs. I hold them together tightly. He finds his resistance as he grips my hips and thrusts between my contracted thighs. My sex aches for him, *which it's a relief to know I still desire Lance, I still desire our lovemaking,* fear is not winning, *but this sexual act will have to do for now.*

"I'm cumming baby."

"Release against my belly." Lance removes his penis from between my thighs. He urgently jacks himself off and finds his release ejaculating the warm semen against my stomach and thighs. I massage the thick warm liquid into my chest, thighs, and stomach. Lance looks at me bewildered and perplexed. "I need the feel of your semen on me, not his." Lance gets it. *He gets me.* The prince who rescued me only a few

G.L. Ross

hours ago now assists massaging his warm sperm across my skin. His lips press to mine and I briefly forget the pain as we deepen our kiss. Lance's bridled passion is released as his hands slide all over my body, his tongue searches, licks, and enjoys my entire mouth. *Yes, there is pain, but this is what I need. I feel like a woman and not a victim.* Lance rinses us both before drying and wrapping me in a thin, white towel. After he dries and dresses, my prince heroically carries me back to the narrow hospital bed. *He insists he carry me. Who am I to complain?*

Free from all sin and filth I allow myself to sleep peacefully knowing my *boyfriend* is by my side spooning and protecting me. *My boyfriend, my Prince Charming, by my side for always and forever.*

Turbulent Passion

Chapter Fourteen

Horny Bastard

It's been five days since I brought Lisa home from Austin. Rather than having her face people in the airports or on the plane I rented a car and drove us to Dallas. We went by her parents first so she could tell them what happened and they could see, for themselves, she was alright. Her family seemed to approve of me and agreed if she wouldn't stay with them then she should stay with me. *I had my fingers crossed and said a small prayer she would chose me, which she did.*

Caring for Lisa has been heartwarming. She transforms my house into a home. She injects warmth and love throughout. I love having her here, with me, beside me. We arrived late the first night, so she was unable to view the outside landscaping. I explained while staying here she has free reign of the first floor, but I don't want her climbing stairs yet to explore the second level. *Thank goodness the master bedroom is on the first floor.*

G.L. Ross

Waking up in my bed with Lisa in my arms puts a smile on my face and pep in my step. *Corny, huh? But true.*

"Lance, you really don't need to…"

"Hush," I say with my finger pressed against her pouty lips. "I want to."

Slowly, so very slowly, I ease my body down Goddesses. My tongue teases her nipple as my fingers plump her beautiful breasts. My tongue traces across her chest and ribs, stopping briefly to dip inside her navel, before my kisses drift from hip to hip. My hands slide under her beautiful ass and my moist tongue slides through her cleft. She tenses and moans twisting my insides out. I suckle and tease her clit. She grips the sheets with her fingers and I find myself hard, erect, and aching for her wet heat. I lift her hips and place her legs over my broad shoulders. *I love the way she is spread wide for me.* My mouth engulfs her sex, tasting her sweet heat against my eager tongue and lips. Her head tosses back and forth frantically, she moans and begs for more and then in her euphoric state begs me to stop. Lisa is undone *and I love it.* I catch her observing my tongue lick

Turbulent Passion

and tease her. Her glazed look melts me. I love seeing Lisa lose it under my touch and command. Lightly *and teasingly* I blow air against her bulging button before sucking it deeply inside my warm mouth. The two extremes send Lisa's hips bucking against my lips. My arms stretch forward permitting my fingers the capability to tantalize and pinch her hardened nipples. Her legs straighten and her body tenses. "Lance, Lance, oh my…."

"Let go, Lisa." I lift and squeeze her firm ass. "Cum now," I order before my tongue plunges fully into her wet erogenous zone. My thumb circles and presses against her pulsing clit. She screams and explodes against my tongue. "Good girl, baby." I lick, kiss, and bite my way up to her delicious mouth. "Now, that is how you begin a great day."

****

I greet my gorgeous Goddess at the back door with a lovely bouquet of white roses and dark purple calla lilies, which happen to be her absolute favorites. "Hi baby, I missed you," she seductively mutters, before leaning forward for a brief kiss.

G.L. Ross

"These are for you, gorgeous." I hand her the bouquet, before dropping the six grocery bags I'm juggling.

"Lance, they are beautiful and my favorites. You really shouldn't have. But, I'm so glad you did," she giggles. *Score one for the wooing boyfriend.* She blushes as she asks, "Did you pick up my prescription?" *Why is she embarrassed about birth control pills?* Especially after everything we have shared?

I unload my arms and lean against the counter. I spread my legs and motion for my sexy green-eyed Goddess to come to me. "Yes, I did, I also picked up the results from my blood tests, which happen to be clear, and as far as your other statement by all means allow me to spoil my girl with flowers or whatever I so choose. Now give me a real kiss and stop blushing." Her kisses are pure perfection.

We put away the groceries together, as a real couple would do, and I am happy, truly happy being domestic, living a simple life. I am beyond happy having Lisa here with me twenty-four hours a day. I can't stand not being able to make love to her, but I

Turbulent Passion

don't want to injure her either. "Lisa, when did the doctor say we could have sex, not oral, but the whole shebang?"

"The whole shebang?" she giggles. "Is someone frisky, baby?" She loves playing with me. *She knows she holds all the power.*

"Beyond frisky, I am at full fledge horny." I grab her hips and pull her against my chub. "This is what you do to me."

She smiles, flashes her long, luscious lashes and coos, "The doctor said five to seven days."

"So, we are at five and a half, almost six right now?" I rub my jeans against her shorts, easily finding her cleft.

"Why yes, sir, we are." She nibbles my ear lobe and I lose all control.

I hurriedly sweep her into my arms, carry her into the bedroom, toss her on the bed, and bam, clothes begin flying through the air. *Literally we rip each other's clothes off.* We are ravenous to be

G.L. Ross

physically connected, to be one. It's so spontaneous and savage - I love it. *She loves it, too.*

I crawl towards the center of the bed and recline on my back. I urge Lisa to crawl on top. I'm extremely aroused and definitely don't want to hurt her. "You are in control. Take it as slow as you need, love. I'm serious. I don't want to hurt you." I position my hips so she is able to ease onto me, after applying the condom. *I will be glad when the pills are back to full strength. Our blood work is clear, so very soon we will be barrier free.*

My burning, black eyes sweep up and down her curvaceous body. I crave this woman. She begins a languid ride, up and down, leaning forward into me as I taught her, so she receives ultimate pleasure. I moan as I grab her breasts squeezing and pinching her erect nipples. *I almost forgot how incredible it feels to be inside her.* It's actually unimaginable, indescribable. Other women didn't feel like this – not even close.

Our orgasms build quickly. She bucks against me. "Give me more, Lance. I'm fine. I can handle it. I need every inch of you."

Turbulent Passion

I eagerly thrusts upward. She rides me faster and faster, begging me to go deeper and harder. I finally toss her over to her back. She giggles as I push her legs up and out driving myself relentlessly into her. She urges me again, "Faster baby, faster - harder Lance."

"Damn you are a demanding handful," I laugh.

"Lance, go deeper baby, go deeper." Her nails dig into my firm, clenched ass, pulling me closer. *God, I have missed this.* She cries out my name as we find our release simultaneously. A moment later I collapse against her staying deep inside her. I never want to leave her, ever.

I'm still inside her as she pants, "Lance that was beyond incredible, that was mind-blowing. I have missed us, like this."

"Me too, baby. I'm glad I can impress and please you." I roll to my back and toss the condom into a nearby trash basket. *Hate those things.*

G.L. Ross

Lisa curls under the nook of my arm placing her head on my heaving chest. "You always please me Lance. I hope I will always please you."

"Well the fact you are my Goddess pleases me." I squeeze her tight ass cheek, before rolling her over to start again.

We have many days to make-up and I am a horny bastard. LOL.

Faithful Friend

Two days ago I returned to flying. Everything has gone well except for Lance's constant texts and calls to check on me. I shouldn't complain. He loves me and I love him, which is what I've always wanted. Admittedly I didn't want it at this point in my life, but that's what I get for making plans which are really in God's hands. Perhaps someday soon I will have the nerve to tell him how much I love and adore him. I wouldn't have survived my ordeal had it not been for Lance's strength and enduring love.

Turbulent Passion

"Lisa, this is Stephen, please give me a call. It's important." I wonder what could be wrong. This is the thing I hate about cross country flights, Stephen left that message four hours ago and I'm only now able to listen and return the call.

"Stephen, hey it's Lisa, what's up? You sounded worried."

"Lisa, Terri had complications in delivery."

"Oh my gosh, the baby. It is March, so the baby is on time, not premature. What happened? Are Terri and the baby okay?" I'm rambling like an idiot.

"The baby is fine, it's a boy." I release my held breath.

"Congrats! I am so excited for you."

Stephen begins to cry. "Thanks Lisa. I am so scared. I can't lose her."

I've never heard Stephen scared or upset. "Stephen please tell me what is going on?"

"Terri is in the ICU. She lost a lot of blood. They had to do a hysterectomy. She is going to be so

G.L. Ross

upset, but I just want her to live, to be okay. I need her." My heart breaks for my pleading friend. I want so badly to hold him and make everything alright. He has always been there for me, whether blubbering about a guy or screaming about school. Stephen is always there and deserves everything his heart desires. He is one of the good guys.

"Of course you do, I am sure she will be fine. She has doctors and nurses there to give her the very best care. I'll say a prayer, for both of you."

"Thanks Lisa."

"I land in Dallas tonight. What hospital should I come to?"

"You will come?" Poor Stephen, he sounds like a frightened child.

"Of course, I wish I could be there right now."

Appearing to calm his staggered breathing he briskly continues, "Tonight is fine. We are at Presbyterian Dallas Medical Center. Come to the 4th

Turbulent Passion

floor for Maternity. I will be in the ICU waiting room."

"It will be around midnight, but I will be there."

"Thanks Lisa. I love you." My heart swells.

"I love you, now be strong."

I need to be there for my dear friend. Loyal friends are hard to find and should be absolutely cherished. My heart hurts for him.

Passengers begin boarding the plane for our flight to Dallas. I have to get a quick, silent prayer in for Stephen and Terri, "Lord, please take care of Terri. Wrap your loving arms around Terri, Stephen, and their son. Stephen needs a wife and this boy deserves a mom. Place your healing hands on Terri. Give Stephen strength to accept whatever your will may be. Amen."

"Welcome to Dallas/Fort Worth. Please remain seated with your luggage stowed while we taxi to the gate." Why is it passengers take forever to stow their luggage when they board, but are so quick

G.L. Ross

to deplane? Probably the same reason people need wheelchairs when they pre-board, but they are suddenly healed when we land. People watching is quite entertaining.

"Bye Lisa, hope your friend's wife is okay."

While walking to my car I shout my response, "Thanks Kathy. I enjoyed flying with you. Thanks for being so sweet and helpful."

"My pleasure. You take care of yourself and tell Lance, hi!"

"Will do." No messages from Stephen; I guess "no news is good news." Presbyterian isn't far from the airport; in fact, it's actually on my way home. I really hope Terri is okay.

Hate is a strong emotion, but I seriously hate parking in hospital parking lots, especially at night. It is truly creepy. It reminds me of a scene from a scary movie. I keep waiting for someone to jump out and grab me. *Did I mention I hate scary movies?*

Okay, talked myself through that journey, now where is the elevator? This place is enormous.

Turbulent Passion

"Hold the elevator please," I holler. An elderly, smiling man is standing in the elevator. "Thank you sir; do you mind pushing floor four for me?"

"No problem, mam."

Mam? I am a mam? Man these mid to late twenties must have aged me.

"Who do you fly for mam?" I inwardly laugh and cringe due to the matronly three letter word.

"International Air."

"Love that airline. Y'all are so friendly."

"Well I am pleased to hear that. Here I am 4th floor. Have a nice evening sir."

"You too, mam."

Jeez, I really am not digging this mam thing. "Excuse me, could you direct me towards the ICU waiting room?"

"Yes mam." *Not again*! "Down the hall and to the left."

G.L. Ross

Irritation *and tiredness* get the best of me as I decide to dish it back to the monotone nurse. "Thank you, *mam*." Wonder how she likes it? Of course, she looks as though she is in her forties, *so she is a mam.*

I find Stephen in the ICU waiting room, bless his heart he has fallen asleep in the most awkward position. His neck is going to kill him tomorrow or today I should say. I hate to wake him, but I will be rescuing his neck. "Stephen, Stephen." Guess whispering isn't going to work; I will have to shake him. "Stephen."

"What's wrong? I am here Terri!" Crap, I have startled him.

"Stephen, it's okay. It's me. Nothing is wrong."

"Oh, thank goodness. Lisa I'm so happy to see you." My dear, sweet friend jumps to his feet and wraps me in a bear hug. *Wow, what a hug.* I can barely breathe.

"Stephen, sit down and let me get you a cup of coffee."

Turbulent Passion

"No Lisa I'm fine." I give him one of my looks and he slowly lowers to the muted beige chair.

"Stephen it is one o'clock in the morning. I need a cup of coffee and I know you do, too."

"Lisa let me get them." Stephen starts to stand, but I push his shoulders lowering him back to the chair.

"You trying to steal my job? Coffee, tea, or me?" I give Stephen one of my playful grins, throw my hands on my hips, and he finally cracks a smile. "Glad to know I can still make you smile cowboy."

"Yes you can and I believe I will take all three." He's still able to tease and flirt with me, even in this situation. "Thanks for being here Lisa. I knew you, of all people, could make me calm down."

"My pleasure, I will be right back." It does makes you feel warm inside when you can help someone. *I like this feeling.* Locating the break area I find the coffee machine. Guess I had better brew a fresh pot, who knows how long that sludge has been sitting.

G.L. Ross

"Code red, code red, room 421."

Man, look at them take off. Hope that isn't Terri's room. Maybe I should go see. No, it looks as though they are running in a different direction. Wonder if there are any cute doctors? *My mom would be thrilled if I brought home a doctor.* Of course, I don't think I would want to date an OB/GYN. I want my "girlie parts" to be the only "girlie parts" my man sees. *I really need to stop talking to myself.* Besides, I have Lance. The thought of my magnificent man makes me smile as wide as Texas.

"Sorry it took so long, Stephen. I brewed a fresh pot. You do still take it black, right?"

"Yes mam." Nails on a black board!

"Oh please Stephen, not you too."

Startled by my exclamation he challenges, "What did I say?"

"Nothing really, it's just I have been called mam all day and my Mom is a mam, *not* me!"

Turbulent Passion

Laughing and relaxing in his straight back, extremely uncomfortable chair Stephen sinks into conversation. "Lisa, I love you. You are the rainbow after the storm."

"You, dear sir, are entirely too sweet. I am happy to help. Hey Teri isn't in room 421, is she?"

"No, she is in 443, which is the ICU area. But the doctor came by and said she has improved they hope to move her to a regular room in a few hours." The relief in his face and shoulders is a welcome surprise.

"That is great news, Stephen." Staring upward I mouth, "Thank you Lord Jesus."

"Exactly, thank you Lord. Why did you ask about 421?"

"They had a code red when I was making coffee. They all ran to room 421."

"Oh, hope they're okay, whoever it is. I feel for anyone going through this hell on earth. I have never been so scared in my entire life."

G.L. Ross

"Well it's over now. Are your parents or Terri's parents here?"

"No, they all arrive tomorrow. Maybe then I can go home, take a shower, and get some rest. I really hope Terri isn't devastated about the hysterectomy." My heart breaks for both of them, but at least they are blessed with a healthy, baby boy.

"Stephen, she will be disappointed and probably depressed at first, but she'll eventually accept it and be thankful for the child you two have been gloriously blessed with. I think that it will be good for you to go home and sleep. It will also be good for Terri to spend some time with her mom to discuss the hysterectomy. I'm glad her mom is coming." On a lighter note, "You do realize you won't be sleeping much now that…what did you name your son?"

"Connor," he proudly says with a smile.

"Strong name. No sleep for you now that Connor is here. Where is that son of yours? I think it's time he meets his Auntie Lisa."

Turbulent Passion

Walking to my car, all I can think about is precious Connor. I'm so happy for Stephen and Terri. I can't believe it is four in the morning though. I didn't feel right leaving Stephen until Terri was moved to her new room. I'm glad he has a recliner to sleep in; maternity rooms are very plush these days. Plus all the new grandparents will be arriving soon, so Stephen needs a nap.

Is that my phone buzzing? Crap, four text messages. Hospitals have the lousiest reception.

First message: "Lisa, call me. Love ya, Lance." Oops forgot to call.

Second message: "I looked at your screen. I know you landed. Please call me."

Third message: "Where are you? Call me." Jeez Louise, he's worried.

Fourth message: "Are you okay? Don't do me this way Lisa. Call me, before I head your way." What the - When I get home I will deal with him. Men!

G.L. Ross

Driving home has given me time to simmer and get ticked off and concerned. I understand his protectiveness after everything we've been through, but how dare he speak to me that way. I know he is worried, but his control is a bit over the top. I'm exhausted and really don't want to deal with Mr. Control Freak. Honestly, I think I'll bypass the shower and taking off my make-up. I want to put on my pajamas, crawl into bed, and text the insane, possessive, control freak.

Before texting him, I change into my comfy pj's and crawl beneath my warm comforter. *What to say…*

"Who do you think you are? *Never* speak to or text me that way. I appreciate your concern, but not your tone. I was at the hospital with a friend and apparently had lousy cell reception. I am now going to bed at almost five in the morning, so do not call me." *That should take care of him.* I am turning my phone off and going to sleep. *Men, men, men.*

Bathroom! I think my bladder is going to burst. I hate it when my bladder wakes me from a wonderful sleep. What time is it anyway? Eight AM?

Turbulent Passion

I can't believe I'm awake. Stupid bladder. *Must be the frickin' coffee.*

Where is my phone? Let's see if Mr. Control responded.

One voice message: "Lisa, thank you so much for coming to the hospital last night. Terri is much better and Connor is great. We are lucky to have you as a friend. Terri says thank you for keeping me calm. We love you." He is the sweetest. *I really should have dated him.*

Hmm, not sure what to think about not receiving a message from Lance. He definitely has a temper and always has to be in control. Maybe he is off pouting. *What the hell is that banging?* Are my neighbors fighting again?

"Lisa, open the damn door!" *Oh shit!*

G.L. Ross

Turbulent Passion

Chapter Fifteen

Control Freak

"Stop that incessant beating," Lisa shrieks while opening her apartment door. I jerk her into my arms, thank goodness she is okay; desiring the delectable taste of her mouth I lower my lips briefly hesitating as though waiting for her invitation. *Which I don't necessarily need.* How dare she worry me? Under my command she responds by parting her lips. The teasing game I'm playing assaults her senses. Her breathing rapidly becomes a pant, *for me. Good, she deserves to succumb to my will after scaring the shit out of me!*

On the verge of grabbing and taking what I desire, I abruptly stop and choose to deny her any continued pleasure. "So, you forgot to call or text me? You knew I asked you to let me know when you were home safely. You knew I would worry. You should be punished."

"Punished, Lance? I think not. If you want to get technical I did text you when I was safely home," she smarts off. I feverishly slam my mouth to hers. Our teeth clash. I tilt my head diving and

G.L. Ross

swirling my devilish tongue inside her marvelous mouth. *This woman frustrates me!* Swiftly I pull my head back while cupping her face in my hands. Her reaction tells me my eyes frighten her. They are no doubt dilated and black. My teeth latch and pull on her pouty, bottom lip. I reach between her thighs and feel a moist heat. A purring sound seeps from my mouth that sparks and ignites her engine. Pressing my hips to her body, I allow her to feel the large, growing bulge pressing against the zipper of my slacks.

I nuzzle her slender neck enjoying her sweet, vanilla scent. "You smell so good and you have been so bad," I growl. Sternly I stare into her hungry eyes and with one quick, fluid motion I sweep and cradle her in my strong arms. She giggles and nuzzles my cheek on the way into her bedroom. Lisa's engine is vibrating and ready for my onslaught. I lower her to the bed leaning forward, for one last luscious taste of her swollen lips. She eagerly leans back on her elbows ready for my large, excited frame to drive her delirious. Instead I sit in a chair, near the bed. Dear Miss Price is baffled and sexually frustrated. *Welcome to my world, sweetheart.*

Turbulent Passion

In a completely confused and bewildered state she sits upright beseeching me, "What's wrong? Aren't you going to join me in bed?" My baby is pouting like an adoring child who lost their favorite toy.

"Not yet. You owe me an apology. Strip for me, Lisa."

Miss Price picks her jaw up off the floor before addressing me, "As in undress, while you watch, and why do I owe you an apology?" *I love when she gets riled.*

"Yes, but do it sexually, as though you are seducing me. I want a show. As for the apology, because you caused me to unnecessarily worry about you." She stands in a conundrum. "Do you understand, Lisa?"

"I think. So, like a stripper?" Lisa appears somewhat excited, by my request. *She would never admit that though.*

"Let's not use the word stripper. You are putting on a show for your extremely worried boyfriend." I lean back in the chair, threading my

G.L. Ross

fingers together and placing them behind my head. "Any day now, Lisa," I urge with a half-smile.

"This is really out of my comfort zone, but I will *try* for you. I am sorry you were worried." Is she being sarcastic or sincere? I can't quite tell from her tone. *She is such a smart ass at times, which is part of why I adore her.*

"Good, because you know if you really care for me you want to please me, not worry me. So Lisa, show me how much you care for me. Demonstrate for me how sorry you are for your actions." My voice is deep and raspy. My eyes are dilating once again. I can tell she has absolutely no clue what to do. I doubt Lisa has ever seen a stripper. *My sweet, innocent Goddess.*

She begins swaying her hips. Her hands run up and down her delectably delicious body. *I can't help but smile.* She lifts her sleep shirt over her head, and then teases me by pulling the shirt between her thighs, before tossing it to me. *Lisa is actually pretty good at this.* She covers her tits with her hands. One perky breast is teasingly flashed and re-covered. *Lisa*

Turbulent Passion

is enjoying herself. This is kind of fun. *We may need to play this game often.*

My bulge is rapidly growing. I unbutton and unzip my slacks, for relief. Lisa turns her back to me. She chooses to bend over with her legs straight as she slowly lowers her panties. She peers through those sexy legs of hers and notices I have removed all of my clothing. I am sitting in the chair, blissfully naked, playing with my growing, needy erection. Lisa's mouth drops, *along with her panties,* to the floor. She fastidiously regains composure prior to turning to face me and then she *purposely, wickedly,* licks her lips. *Damn this woman is hot!*

I motion for her to come to me. "Turn around Lisa and lower yourself slowly. I need to be inside your sweet heat."

This is a new position for Lisa. I want to introduce her to all positions. I want to show her how to increase her pleasure and mine. I hold her hips as she repositions my cock against her tension-filled opening. With her back to me, she does as she is told, easing her sex on to my long, full, throbbing hard on. "Oh my, Lance."

G.L. Ross

"Take your time baby."

She accepts my wide crown with a groan. "You are so huge."

"You did this to me, baby." I whisper against her ear, "It's all your fault."

"Remind me to be bad more often," she giggles. I smack her ass before gripping her hips tighter. "Ouch," she bellows.

"Hush now." I direct her to slide up and down on me carefully inching me inside her wet, tight tunnel. I tilt my hips to enable my girth to rub her magic spot.

"This feels good, Lance," she coos.

"I knew you would like it. It helps reach your G-spot." I am going to introduce you to all kinds of fun, my gorgeous Goddess.

"Well it feels incred...Oh my...Lance...Lance."

"Don't be afraid of the intensity. Relax and go with it. Release your tension." Her legs briefly

Turbulent Passion

turn languid before tensing and straightening. She is blown away by the response of her body. "Focus Lisa on the pleasure." I'm still pumping forcefully into her tight, sweet cunt.

I reach around front to grab her bouncing breasts. I love watching her tits bounce. I tease her taut peaks. *She loves when I play with her hypersensitive nipples.* With an arm wrapped around her shapely waist, I pull her back against me. I grind into her, while shamelessly tormenting her clitoris. "Your button is bulging, baby." She tosses her head back against my shoulder. I revel in her pleasure. "I turn you on, don't I Lisa? Are you sorry for worrying me?" She pants but doesn't answer. I abruptly stop playing with her clitoris and instruct her, "Stand up and lean over your chest of drawers."

She stands and obeys. I slap her sassy bottom. "Are you sorry, Lisa?"

Startled, she jumps. "Yes," she pants.

"Do you want me to make you cum?"

"Yes, please yes," she begs.

G.L. Ross

"Then promise you will never disobey me again." She reaches to touch herself. I slap her other cheek. "Put that hand away. Promise me you will obey, Lisa, or else you will not be allowed to cum."

"I promise," she whimpers.

"You promise what?" I slap her other cheek. I love the pink on her apple shaped ass.

"Oh God, make me cum," she whines.

I slap the other a bit harder. She yelps before agreeing, "I promise to obey. Please Lance." I smile and rub her sweet, pink cheeks before pushing her head down and driving hard into her. It's harder and deeper than any time she has experienced, but she is dripping wet which allows me to enter and slide easily.

"Lance, this is really intense." She gasps for air in between my surges. I tuck my arm around to rub her pulsing clit. She is incredibly tight.

"Good, then hold on love." I thrust into her so hard she begins to quake. Her tightening pulse on my dick causes me to mercilessly thrash her. I am beyond turned on as I grab and pull her hair. I love Lisa submitting to me. "Almost there Lisa, hold on baby." I continue barking orders while pulling her hair so I may observe her face, "Push back into me, and cum when I cum. Now Lisa, now." *I adore her orgasm face.* Ordering Lisa as my submissive is the sexiest thing I've ever experienced. We detonate together, "Yes baby, *yes!*" Lisa literally trembles and bucks from the chest of drawers.

"Lance, Oh God, Lance." She stretches and collapses on top of the oak chest.

I fall against her heaving body. I thread my fingers into her damp hair. While massaging her scalp I pant lovingly in her ear, "I love making love to you."

Grecian Goddess

"Lucy, I am a nervous wreck and I don't know why. I'm going to Lance's place for dinner, which shouldn't be a big deal. I stayed there for nearly a week."

G.L. Ross

"Maybe because it feels more like a real date. You guys haven't had the most traditional of relationships."

I'm listening to Lucy while staring at my jam packed closet. Every outfit I try on is wrong. What do you wear for a man who makes your insides shiver? A man who is ripped, hard, broad, tall, with a gorgeous six pack that leads to the sensational V that heats my core until my synapses short out and sizzle. *Seriously, what clothing is appropriate for all that manhood?*

"He wants to make me dinner." I continue ripping clothes from hangers. "There has to be something in my closet that is appropriate to wear for Lance."

"That would be either a black lace teddy or a trench coat with nothing underneath." Lucy laughs as I crumple on my bed and curl into a fetal position.

"You are *not* helping! Not At All," I exclaim.

Turbulent Passion

"Breathe Lisa. Remember you are in control. He is already happy because you agreed to spend time with him. You call the shots."

"I need about three shots of tequila." After a few deep breaths I return to my closet in search of the perfect outfit. "Lucy, the problem is I'm not in control when Lance gazes into my eyes, or nuzzles my neck, or even when I smell his cologne. I become one huge, pulsing hormone. A hormone which craves Lance."

"Then stop craving and start enjoying."

"Excuse me?"

"You heard me. Stop fighting your feelings. Have fun, Lisa. He obviously adores you and has admitted to loving you. I think it's time you lower some of your walls and allow yourself to fall in love."

Fifteen minutes later Lucy and I are still talking as I stand in front of my full length mirror admiring an outfit. "Maybe you're right. Maybe I do need to relax and have fun. But, I don't think I can endure a broken heart, especially after all I have been

G.L. Ross

through in the last few weeks. I said I would not date a pilot and what do I do? I date the biggest player pilot at the airline, who you told me to stay away from, if you recall." *Should I trust him with my heart?*

Lucy continues offering more advice, "I know I warned you about him, but he isn't the manwhore he used to be." *Well isn't that nice.* "He is a different man, since you came into his life. He has changed because of you. Steve Harvey says a man will only change for one woman. You are Lance's one woman, Lisa. Follow your gut, rather than the ache between your legs. Your gut tried to warn you about Wayne. Listen to your gut and you will be fine. Guarantee."

"Guarantee?" I want a guarantee that protects my heart.

"Yes mam. You are smart Lisa. Your heart will guide you. Now choose an outfit and get dressed, wear something sexy, but that covers, so he has to imagine. Men enjoy intrigue. They are visual. Also, grab a bottle of wine. You don't want to show up empty handed."

Turbulent Passion

"Got it. Thanks Lucy." I turn on the shower and grab a couple of oversized, fluffy, white towels.

"Remember I get the first phone call in the morning. I expect a play by play."

"Absolutely. Thanks for the advice. Hope you have a great evening."

"You too." I hear the smart ass in her voice.

Lucy is a true blessing. I'm quite fortunate to have a friend who is able to give me advice about relationships and sex. Talk about turning the tables, here I am the counselor receiving advice rather than giving, but it's really different reasoning with yourself.

Okay, stop talking to yourself and get in the shower. Prince Charming awaits.

I arrive at Lance's home at 7 PM sharp; although, home seems entirely inadequate when describing Lance's *castle*. I knew the address was a Highland Park address, which is one of the nicest areas in Dallas, but I never expected *this*. His place covers two lots and is a two story Austin Stone home,

G.L. Ross

which I love. The door is a double door at least ten feet high, the lawn is professionally landscaped, and in the courtyard is a gorgeous marble fountain. I knew his house was lovely inside, but I never realized the outside was over-the-top phenomenal.

How on earth does he afford this? Pilots make good money, *but not this kind of money.*

Before knocking on the door, I decide to get a closer view of the fountain. The marble is a lovely jade green. The water flows from an urn held by a lady draped in what appears to be a toga. I think it's Grecian. Her face carries a slight smile, but it is her eyes that magnetically pull me towards her.

His deep, dusty voice startles me. "Do you like?"

I scream, "Oh my gosh." I juggle the bottle of wine resting in my arms. Fortunately, Lance reacts quickly and catches it before it crashes against the ground. "You startled me. I didn't hear you. Say something next time!"

"Yes mam, chill Lisa. Everything is okay. I was in the backyard when you pulled in so I came

Turbulent Passion

through the pass way to greet you. You were so deep in thought you didn't hear my approach. Although, I thoroughly enjoyed watching you." His sexy smile erases the last few minutes. I find myself hypnotized by his sky blue eyes and brazen gaze. *I adore this man.*

"Nice save with the wine," I calmly reply. *Nice change of tone, Lisa.* His smile always relaxes me.

"I believe I deserve a reward." *Yes, please.*

My voice abandons my control and turns low and sultry. "What did you have in mind?"

"This…" Lance wraps one arm around my shoulder and pulls me against his hard as iron chest. His soft lips lower to mine. My sex clenches. His touch sizzles. The kiss begins chastely, but his scent and warmth overwhelm me. Heat spreads under my skin. My lips slightly part. Lance slips his tongue between my lips. My nipples pucker against the brush of his chest. I tilt my head ever so lightly to deepen his taste. The licks inside my mouth stroke the fire growing inside me. Just as I expected…I am

G.L. Ross

soaked…going, going… *gone.* This man unravels me.

"Perhaps we should move this inside. I don't care to give my neighbors a free peep show." He lovingly places a kiss on my forehead.

He has no idea the control he has over my body.

"I really do love your fountain."

"Thanks. I commissioned a Dallas artist to make her when I bought the house." His heated gaze undresses me. I lust, *outright lust* for his touch, his body.

"Is she a Grecian goddess?" I unintentionally growl.

"Perhaps, he titled her *The Green Goddess*." In the back of my mind I recall Lance using the term "Goddess" many times when referencing me. He must have a thing for green-eyed Goddesses. I have a thing for sculpted blue-eyed men who love fucking me. *Did I just use the "F" word?* Man, I really do lose all control with him.

Turbulent Passion

As we enter Lance's not so humble abode, I am completely blown away, again. The interior is something out of *Architectural Digest* and *Interior Design* magazines. "Lance, your home really is stunning."

"Thank you, but the loveliest part of my home is you standing inside it." His hand slides to the nape of my neck. His eyes burn into mine. "The house and I have both missed you." *Okay, he is good...very good indeed.* "Let's head into the kitchen. I have a bottle of wine breathing." *I'm glad something is breathing.*

An incredible aroma floats towards me as we enter a kitchen fit for a professional chef. All of the appliances are top notch, the cherry cabinets exude warmth, even the refrigerator door is covered in cherry wood. Lance hands me a glass of wine and pulls out a bar stool for me to sit upon. "Thank you, sir." *There is nothing better than a true gentleman.*

"My pleasure. I really am pleased we are having an official date." I sip my wine and search for the right words. Thank goodness Lance continues chatting, "I figured we could visit while I complete

G.L. Ross

the final touches of our dinner. So, have you missed me?" Look at that grin. A boyish charm inhabits my insatiable man.

"Lance, it has only been a few days." Lance leans across the counter presenting a wooden spoon full of rich, tomato sauce.

He blows on it, before placing it to my lips. "What do you think?" I think I just had an orgasm from homemade marinara being served to me. *How does he make everything seductive?*

"That is incredible. Did you make it?"

"Of course. You think I am going to serve you marinara from a jar? I have many hidden talents, Lisa." Honestly, yes, I would have served you sauce from a jar *and oh do I know about your many talents.*

Gorgeous and cooks, not to mention his sexual prowess, how on earth did I snag this man? "Where did you learn to cook?"

"After high school I toured Italy and France. The family I stayed with had an incredibly talented

Turbulent Passion

cook, whom I adored, so Abigail taught me how to create Italian cuisine."

"She taught you well."

"Do you like the wine?"

"Yes, very much," I reply. "What brand is this?"

Lance places the green glass bottle beside my wine goblet. I begin to read the fancy scripted label when it dawns on me… "Miller's Magic? Miller - as in Lance Miller?"

Lance's eyes begin to dance. "Yes, mam. I am relieved and pleased you approve of my wine."

"Lance is this how you are able to own this castle?"

Lance chokes, laughs, and sputters, "Castle?"

"Well, home doesn't seem to truly encompass this …this…estate?"

G.L. Ross

"I don't believe estate is appropriate either, but I am pleased you like my *home*." I eagerly stare at him urging him to continue with his financial extravagance explanation. "My grandfather owned several wineries in Italy and France. My father inherited the wineries, but chose to hire managers to run them. He and mom moved to the US before I was born. Dad became involved in the oil industry and is a major player in alternative clean energy. I took control of the wineries about five years ago and still use the presently in place management teams. I visit once a quarter."

"Aren't you full of surprises? So, the wineries afford you this luxury?" I motion my arms in the air.

"Yes, along with a trust fund, stock, and my pilot salary." I sit silently soaking in all of the shared information. "Lisa, it's only money."

"Just money, huh? Easy for you to say, since you have it." *I can't believe I didn't notice the wine last week.* "So, why do you fly? Why not live in Italy?" Lance motions me to follow him as he carries plates heaped with Italian amore. His dining table is

Turbulent Passion

Old World style, with an emerald green tapestry runner gracing the center. Lance's china is solid white, which is what I would expect from Lance's personality. His crystal is quite simple, but elegant and heavy. Il Divo serenades us as we dine by candlelight. After pulling out my chair, Lance places an emerald green linen napkin in my lap. Never in my wildest dreams would I have expected *all of this* from the *flyboy*.

Lance continues his explanation, "I fly Lisa because I enjoy it. Flying is exhilarating and fills a void inside me. I choose to live in the US to be near my family. Perhaps when my parents pass I will move to Italy full time, but that is no time soon. Besides, if I hadn't become a pilot I wouldn't have met you." I blush as Lance laces his fingers with mine. *Somehow this man heats my core with a simple glance.*

"I would love to meet your parents some time."

"Someday," he clips. "I have no doubt they would love to meet you," he continues with a strained tone.

G.L. Ross

I interrupt the tension saturated air by redirecting the conversation. "The shrimp marinara is incredible. I am quite impressed Mr. Miller."

"I am happy you are pleased Miss Price. It is nice to cook for someone. I enjoyed cooking for you those few days."

"I am sure you have mesmerized many ladies with your culinary skills." *Why did I say that?* Why did I mention other women? *Idiot!*

"No, that is not an accurate assumption." He chooses to set me straight with his terse response, "I have only entertained one other woman, besides you, and she was my realtor. We celebrated the closing on this home."

"You never cease to amaze and embarrass me."

Lance leans back in his chair. He balances his wine glass between two fingers. His gaze electrifies my nerve endings. "I am honored, but why me Lance?"

"Why not you?" he jabs.

Turbulent Passion

"Seriously, Lance, why me?" Lance stands and reaches for my hand. His intense eyes still startle me. I think they always will.

"Dance with me." Hypnotized by his aura I stand and enter his welcoming arms. He nuzzles his face into my hair. The warmth of his breath against my ear sends tingles up and down my spine.

The song couldn't be more appropriate, Thompson Square, *This Life Would Kill Me if I Didn't Have You.* "I love this song Lisa. It reminds me of you." He pulls me closer and entices me with the sway of his hips as he executes his skilled dance moves. I lean in absorbing his spicy male scent. His hands slide into my hair teasing my neck with his fingertips. I sigh and lean into his sensual touch. "Lisa?"

"Yes, Lance?" I am lulled by the meal, the music, and *the man.*

"You do know, like the song says, this life would kill me if I didn't have you in it." He is good. *Very smooth.* "Give me a chance, Lisa. Give us a chance." My lashes flutter, but remain lowered. I'm

G.L. Ross

afraid to peer into his eyes. I'm afraid he'll see the love I harbor for him. The love I'm not ready to proclaim. Instead I slide my hands around his trim waist placing my face firmly against his powerful chest, enjoying his warmth and security.

His heart pulses against my cheek as the next song begins to play. Toby Keith belts out one of my favorites, "*You Shouldn't Kiss Me Like This*." I begin singing along with Toby while enjoying my private moment with Lance. *What did I do to earn the love of this man?* I lift my head and stare longingly into his adoring eyes. After a couple of minutes I share, "You were right about him."

"What?"

"About Wayne, you said he would hurt me that he had a different gal each night."

Lance's fingers stroke softly down the length of my hair. "Lisa, I hate he hurt you. I hate I am right when it caused you such pain." His hands cup my face as he asks, "Why are you bringing this up now?"

Turbulent Passion

"I have been dealing with my feelings and I need to admit I misjudged Wayne *and you*. In order to put him in my past I need to admit you were right, about him. I know it doesn't matter to you that you were right, but I need to say it – out loud to you."

"No one will touch you or hurt you ever again. I won't allow it." Lance wraps me snugly in his arms until the song ends.

Once the music ends I implore Lance for my answer, "Lance, answer me, please. Why me? Why am I different?"

The sincerity in his eyes sucker punches me. I stumble as my knees wobble beneath me. Lance pulls me closer against him tightening his grip around my waist. His hands slide warmth up and down my back, eventually resting on my hips. Lowering his mouth to mine he softly answers against my lips, "Because I love you. I am in *love* with you." My breathing halts. He really loves me, even after *everything*. His tongue traces the outer edge of my lips as his eyes penetrate the depth of my soul.

G.L. Ross

I don't know what to say. *He loves me?* We continue to dance with the solo sounds of Josh Groban. Lance's heart beats against my resting palm.

Lance speaks across the top of my crown, "Lisa, I don't expect you to feel the same."

I retreat to see his face. "Lance, can you be monogamous and faithful? Trust me I am not saying this as an assault. I'm really not sure it's in your DNA to be happy with one woman the rest of your life."

"I can for you. You make me happy. I've never felt like this Lisa." The sincerity in his eyes and voice hit me like a ton of bricks. Visibly stunned I fight back the tears welling in my eyes. I know he cares about me. He has proven that. He may truly love me, but can he be monogamous?

"All these women throw themselves at you and they are experienced. They know how to please you, in ways I am unaware."

"You please me, you and only you, besides what other women? Lisa, you have haunted me all my life." *Haunted him?* "Since meeting you my mind

Turbulent Passion

and heart are full of you and no one else." His hands cup my face. "No one else exists. Please believe me."

If I wasn't already turned on, I am now. I feel the wet heat between my legs. My blood simmers beneath his compelling touch. I have no words to express my true feelings, so I nuzzle against his neck encouraging him, inviting him to seduce me.

Kisses, licks, and exploring hands greedily attack me at every counter, wall, and corner as we journey to his bedroom. The room is full of vanilla scented candles, *my favorite scent*. The lights are set to dim. I break from his hold to survey our romantic surroundings. *I still can't get over the fact his bedroom is the size of my apartment.*

The room is richly and warmly covered in jewel toned fabrics. The sleigh bed's cherry finish sparkles and shines amidst the candlelight. His bed is humongous. *He says it's a California King.*

"Are you pleased?" He asks while caressing the length of my arms.

A menagerie of feelings stirs inside my mind, heart, and flesh. "It is lovely, Lance. I love the

G.L. Ross

candles." The candle flames flicker and jump in unison with the flames of passion licking inside me. At the foot of his masterful bed, I stand overwhelmed by the sexual energy and thoughts whipping through my system as Lance kisses and nuzzles my body. My back leans against his hard, chiseled chest tempting him to take me, to overpower me, to own me. *Please make me yours.*

"We are in no rush. We have all night," he whispers into my ear. His salacious kisses grace and cover my shoulders. "Let's play and build to the moment. Let me build your desire, Lisa." *Please, just plow into me now.*

The ache between my legs is now a very uncomfortable throbbing. "I do adore you, Lance. I want to believe in us. You know that don't you?" I breathlessly stutter.

"Why couldn't we have met years ago when I was still a good guy?" He growls through a clenched jaw.

I turn to face him. The brokenness in his eyes tortures my heart and soul. I embrace him with

Turbulent Passion

all of my unspoken love. "Lance..." His hands brush against the sides of my heavy, engorged breasts, before settling on my waist. "I… treasure you." I can't say love, not yet. Love requires complete trust. *I am not there, yet.*

Lance reads me well and knows not to push. He knows my thoughts and needs instinctively, so he knows in his heart what I feel for him. Without a single word spoken, we quickly undress admiring the true nakedness of each other. Lance has bared his soul verbally. Now I will show him my bare, real, raw feelings, without words. I will express my love the way he and only he has taught me, shown me. His lips press against the nape of my neck in a gentle touch, but something inside me senses a proprietary marking of *his* territory and *I like it.*

He understands my need for security and tenderness, but he also knows I find tenderness in his strength. Knowing exactly what I desire he wraps his arms around me and carries me to his bed, *our bed.* His breath feathers across my heated flesh. His warmth, his love, his scent I absorb deeply into my senses. Lance reaches the woman in me. He makes me feel energized, completely alive.

The urgency of our desire for each other is palpable. We constantly crave each other physically, mentally, emotionally. I want to be cared for and loved. He wants my love exclusively for eternity. I center him. I complete him.

My eyes meet his. His eyes study me, reading my thoughts. An electrical charge in the air crackles and sparks between us, similar to the first time our fingers brushed in the cockpit. I decide it is time I initiate. *Do I have the nerve to say how I feel?* Lance's eyes begin a dance of passion and seduction as I recline on my back and spread my thighs wide. Naked I open myself completely to Lance and his love.

He travels and settles between my thighs. The feel of his flesh against mine is magical. My nipples harden and pucker against the hair of his chest. The thick ridge of his erection slides between my cleft. "Baby, I can't wait any longer to be inside you. Look at me as I enter you, look at me when you cum, see us Lisa, see only us." His turbulent,

Turbulent Passion

passionate kisses claim me. "You have no idea what you do to me, Goddess."

Relief bathes me as he claims all of me. *I am his.* His pulsing shaft is solid steel sliding in and out of me. My eyes roll back as my back arches from the staggering, steady, stroking rhythm. "Lance, I do need you," I pant.

"The feel of being inside your tight cunt consumes me. I've never wanted someone the way I want you. I've never felt I belonged to someone like I do you, but right now being inside you Lisa feels like being home," he grunts and pants, between skilled strokes. My eyes gleam, my heart jumps as he continues to rock in and out of me. I'm enjoying every blessed inch of him as he possesses me. My talented flyboy knows how to drive me to my peak. His hips roll and hit my magic spot repeatedly, with his pulsing, unsheathed, thick ridge.

"Lance, tilt my hips. Plunge deeper and harder into me, please." Wasting no time at all, Lance pulls me to the edge of the bed tossing my legs around his waist. His feet rest on the floor as he

G.L. Ross

relentlessly and ferociously drives deeply into my pulsing kitty.

"Your tight, greedy cunt craves me, baby. Squeeze and milk me," he exclaims. Lance's glistening body tightens. His beautiful ass clenches as he plunders me. I'm amazed as I watch him masterfully work my body and his. Instinctively he tugs and lifts me so his thick crown mercilessly hammers my sweet spot. Once again I arch towards Lance, pressing the purple, pulsing head deep within my fiery furnace. "That's it, Lisa. Christ, you are squeezing me tight. Drain me, baby." My body quakes and tightens. My legs straighten and jerk in the air. Lance grabs my thighs pushing them spread eagle as he jackhammers me. "I want you like this always, for me. Spread open, wet, begging me to make you cum." My body overpowers me. Vibrations erupt throughout my senses. "Lisa, look at me," Lance shouts. My eyes fly wide open as my body continues to bow from the mattress. "Now Lisa, clench me now! Cum for me." My body thrashes and vibrates as I explode under Lance's steely pleasure and commands.

Turbulent Passion

Chapter Sixteen

Dominant

"I love the heat blazing in your eyes." My fingers playfully spread her sunshine inspired locks across the pillows. "I also love the fact you are in my bed looking thoroughly fucked and happy."

Preceded by a laugh she responds, "Your words are so charming and romantic."

"I'll show you romantic. Lie back and spread those gorgeous legs." Lisa happily leaps at my command all quivering and wet, which makes my dick hard, *rock hard*. My tongue laves her pulsing opening. "I love you always being wet and ready for me, baby. I want you to always be aroused by my touch." My kisses tingle against her inner thighs. "Lisa, you're swollen. Why didn't you say something? I should have stretched you before. I'll prime you this time."

"Jeez Lance," she mutters before attempting to close her thighs.

"What's wrong?"

G.L. Ross

"I'm embarrassed and want up and out of here."

"Stop your nonsense. I will always take care of you. It's my duty and pleasure. You have no reason to be embarrassed." I gently push against Lisa's breast lowering her back against the mattress. "Lie back and enjoy," I purr before licking my way through her swollen slit. Four licks later I enjoy the panting, purring sounds coming from my Goddess.

My lips twitch as I steel myself for our upcoming pleasure. I smile and gaze upon my beautiful Goddess. "Baby…"

"Don't stop Lance," she orders with her eyes closed tightly.

"Baby, look at me."

Lisa's eyelashes flicker open. Peering over her pulsing vulva I am tantalized by the glazed look emanating from my sex craved innocent.

In my happy-go-lucky voice I explain, "Lisa, I actually hunger for you, so I am going to eat you, now." *I can't help but smile as she swallows*

Turbulent Passion

hard. I think I just made her cream with my words. "I am going to fuck you with my fingers, then my tongue, and then my throbbing cock. I can make you cum in ways you never imagined, Lisa. You're going to cum against my fingers first, then my tongue, and then my cock while it is buried deep inside you. Okay?"

Dropping her head back against the pillow she breathlessly utters, "Yes, pu-lease." My fingers play her like a drum. I delve in and out of her wet arousal. Long, slow strokes rub against her spongy inner spot causing her luscious body to strain towards me. My thumb kneads and circles her engorged clit.

"That's it baby, press against my hand. It feels good, doesn't it? I love it when you let go. Trust me, Lisa." I plunge a second finger inside her, spreading and stretching her. My fingers tease her sex dipping deep and then shallow. She rolls her hips unwittingly against my hand. I feel her need for friction. *I need my dick deep inside her.*

"Lance," she begs.

G.L. Ross

"What Goddess? Tell me what you need from me."

She reaches to rub herself. "I need to cum and cum hard."

"No, Lisa. You behave." I grip her wrist with one hand while sliding three fingers of my free hand inside her. My fingers scissor stretch her, preparing her for my thick width and length. I glance towards the uncomfortable feeling between my legs and find my throbbing head stretching from my unbelievably hard erection. *I am more than ready for my baby.* "Tell me what you need Lisa. You know the rules."

"To cum," she screams. I curl all three fingers against her sweet spot and massage the spongy tissue until she is in a frenzied state. Tears pool in her eyes. "Please, Lance." I release her wrist and focus my attention on pinching and twisting her stiff, pink peaks. She screams as she unravels against my three curled fingers collapsing limply against the bed searching for air. Being the greedy lover I am, I continue to pulverize her beautiful body with my

Turbulent Passion

tongue. First, my tongue dips into her navel. "Lance, no more. That's enough."

"It's never enough. I can't get enough of you, love." My tongue slips between her crevices and discovers her hypersensitive button. I lick and tease until she rocks from the bed into a sitting position. My licks are devious *and I love it*. She cradles my head with her hands. I feel her sex tightening around my piercing tongue. Her orgasm is coming faster and harder than the last. Lisa loses herself in the painful pleasure. She flops back against the bed and grips the headboard. I pull her legs further apart and lift her hips as I crawl to my knees. I want to be under her skin, in her skin, be her skin; I want us. My tongue dives devilishly into her heated opening. She cries out as I continue my erotic spearing. I feel her body screaming for release. I relish the control I have over Lisa's pleasure. A wildfire is spreading through her body. Goddesses' breathing is ragged, sporadic. She angles her hips pushing her sex closer to my hungry mouth. A storm of emotions whirlwinds through my body. My entire mouth engulfs her sex. I want to own this woman. *She can never belong to anyone else.* I will push her limits so that no one else can ever

G.L. Ross

please her the way I do. My tongue plunders her slick opening, with long, luscious licks. My mouth melds with her throbbing clit. The animalistic moans and thrashing coming from Goddess spirals me out of control; with a final suckling she pushes her pulsating sex against my tongue and tumbles into the fiery embers. *Two down, one to go.*

Desire still beats and pulses between her limp legs. Eager to be inside her scorching furnace I stretch and hover over her. "Lance, I can't," she protests.

I wickedly smile. "Baby, this is my forte'. Lie back and enjoy. I will do all the work." The ruffle of excitement and anticipation in Lisa's eyes encourages me to continue my quest. My crown rest against Lisa's still quaking opening. I tease and build her desire by rocking my hips so I barely enter her notch before pulling out. Lisa's raking gaze devours my throbbing cock. *Her hunger for me will never, ever get old.*

"Put it in, Lance," she growls. Her eyes dance in the glow of the candle flames. I can't help but be turned on by the sexy way she wears the scent

Turbulent Passion

of lust and love. I tilt and enjoy the push of my hard dick sliding slowly inside her sexy heat. "I mean it Lance. Bury yourself in me," she hungrily dictates.

I tease her by going a tiny bit deeper. "Good now, baby?"

"Deeper," she screams. Her nails dig into my ass.

I nestle my hips against hers and cast my eyes upon the beautiful sculpture of her glorious curvaceous body. "Lisa, do you want all of me?"

She digs her nails further into my tightened ass. Ready to own her I thrust as far as I am able. Lisa flinches, before falling into a rhythmic seductive dance between our agile bodies. Masterfully I execute the exact angle to produce a toe curling tempo, for my baby. Her moans ignite an animalistic drive in my core. Clenching muscles in my arms, thighs, and ass quake as my rod rams Lisa's tight channel.

"I am addicted to you, Lisa Price." I continue grinding against her, before sliding forcefully into the woman who owns my love and

G.L. Ross

lust. The tempo continues slow and steady, driving me up and up towards the brink of relinquished control. My nerve endings are raw as Lisa teeter's on the edge. I feel her body tightening beneath me. I expel my order between driving plunges, "Not. Done. Yet. Lisa. Wait. For. Me."

"I have no control, Lance. I'm lost," she cries while reaching to grip the sheets.

I almost lose control watching her thrash under my power. "I have you, Lisa. I will always have you, baby. You are mine." I place my hands under her clenching cheeks and angle her once again. Like a piston, I drive into her beautiful, heated abyss, until we both fall over the stormy, jagged edge called "love."

Submissive

Morning dawns with Lance's thick hard prowess briefly rubbing between my wet lips, before sliding deep inside me. *I had no idea I could become wet in my sleep.* The man has talents, many miraculously, wonderful talents.

Turbulent Passion

"Baby, last night was all about me. Let me take care of you this morning," I urge.

"I am happy right where I am," Lance snickers before slipping my nipple between his teeth.

"Lance," I pout.

"Never say I denied you any pleasure my love. Your wish is my command." Lance pulls out of me, *and I must admit – I'm sad to see him leave*, but I am extremely excited to have his delectable cock inside my greedy mouth. He shifts and repositions himself as my warm mouth envelops his absolutely perfect penis. *Yes, I am aware I have nothing to compare it with, but I can't imagine there is one more perfect.*

"I love the way your hair feels on my body, baby." His fingers run through my golden strands spreading it across his hips and thighs. I pleasure my man until he releases a primal growl and I taste his salty, warm release in my mouth.

Lance disappears into the bathroom as I slowly crawl from *our* disarrayed bedding. There is no way I will forget anytime soon that Lance owns

G.L. Ross

the space between my thighs. I spot his light blue, heavily starched, dress shirt thrown across a chair. I delight in having his scent against my naked body. I feel sexy in his oversized shirt *and nothing else*.

"You are so damn sexy in my shirt," Lance growls in his alpha-male voice.

You are so damn sexy with your flexing, muscular golden chest, abs, and thighs. He is still firm and ready. Does the man stay erect? "Do you like what you see?" I tease.

"Hell yea," he replies in his silky, smooth "I still want to fuck you" voice. *The man has many voices and tones that turn me on in a flash.* Lance laces his fingers with mine and places a kiss on the tip of my nose. "Let's go sit on the couch and visit." *Visit? I thought we were getting ready to try a new position.*

Once we are in the den I dig in my purse for a hairbrush. Right now my hair resembles a tangled tumbleweed. *This is no doubt not my best look.* Lance prepares our coffee and joins me on the couch.

Turbulent Passion

"May I?" he demurely ask, which is not a voice I recognize from Lance's repertoire.

"May you what?" His hand is palm up towards me. *Does he want to dance?*

"Brush your hair - Please." He displays a little boy likeness, with his pouty bottom lip protruding. I can't help but smile and giggle while handing him the boar bristle hairbrush.

"Sure." I turn my back to him so he may wrap his legs around my hips. I feel his erection against my back. *As I mentioned I think it stays erect.* He slowly strokes the brush through my hair. Ever so gently he loosens the tangles. I've always enjoyed my hairdresser blow drying my hair, but Lance stroking my hair is sensual. *Almost orgasmic.* I can't help but recline into his brush strokes. Next thing I know I am wrapped in his arms, curled against his chest, with our legs intertwined. Maybe this is where I belong after all.

****

"Afternoon beautiful." I open my eyes and decide I must be dreaming. A gorgeous, tan, chiseled,

G.L. Ross

sweaty, muscular specimen of man hovers above me. "You going to sleep the day away?" *His smile even makes me wet.*

"It seems every time I wake up, someone wears me out…literally." I pull myself up to lean against the end of the sofa.

"Are you complaining, dear?" Lance stretches and displays his sinewy chest and oh so tempting happy trail. *I adore his V.*

Playful Lance is an absolute favorite shade of my Prince Charming. I reach and grab the waistband of his athletic shorts tugging him towards me. "I will never complain about receiving your undivided attention," I taunt. His lips press warmly against mine. I catch a whiff of work-out Lance's rough, male scent. Even sweaty he turns me inside out. "Have a nice work-out?" I cast my gaze inside his shorts.

Flyboy nuzzles my ear, before answering, "Yes, I did, but I enjoy our work-outs the best."

"Me too, so strip and join me." I climb to my knees and begin pushing his shorts down his

Turbulent Passion

powerful thighs. He steps out of his shorts, but backs away from me. I extend my lower lip and begin to pout.

"Baby, if I join you now we will sleep the rest of the day away."

"And that's bad, why?" My eyes light with excitement, hoping to entice my virile man.

Lance lifts his right eyebrow and smirks, "I'm going to jump in the shower." My eyes light up as I push the afghan, Lance must have covered me with, away. Lance steps back, again. "No mam, you may not join me...this time."

"But, Lance..." Once again I pout as I dejectedly collapse on the sofa.

Lance's long fingers cup my face. His lips softly press against mine as he pulls me to my feet and states, "I left your lunch on the kitchen counter. Go eat and then you may jump in the shower, *after I am finished.* Then we are going for a special drive." He slaps my tush and tells me to, "Hop to it!"

G.L. Ross

Hungrily I stand admiring the fabulous view of his taut, perfect ass exiting the room. *I want to bite it!* He really is yummy *and mine.* "Mine!" I gleefully scream and dance around the room.

My handsome boyfriend, *boyfriend? Hmmm. I think I like the sound of that;* has left me a trio salad plate consisting of fruit, shrimp, and pasta salads. *He really is perfect. Well, as perfect as a man can be.* I carry my plate and glass of water to the granite kitchen bar. While enjoying my salads, I hear my phone ringing in my purse. I hurry to answer it, but by the time I locate it the ringing has stopped. I check my voice messages and hear Lucy ranting away about a trip trade where I could fly with her next week. I remember seeing Lance's laptop somewhere around the kitchen. I need a computer to complete the trade. I search the den, kitchen, and finally find it set up inside his breakfast nook. *This house has entirely too many nooks and crannies. His kitchen is the size of my entire apartment. I know - everything is the size of my apartment.*

I retrieve my plate and glass from the bar and move to sit in the nook area. I hit the power

Turbulent Passion

button, before realizing the computer is already running. It was simply hibernating. The screen loads and mercy me - I am greeted by women wearing strategically placed pieces of leather and lace, with men spanking them. Sexual toys and – devices, for lack of a better word, being sold and described on line, along with sexy outfits for women. The erotic images on Lance's computer intrigue me, *but is Lance into this?*

The visions are interesting, kind of exciting, but also very disturbing. Women being whipped and spanked, sex swings, butt plugs, does Lance get off on this? I wouldn't know where to begin with all of *this.* I search BDSM and find women shackled to beds, posts, and benches. The idea of being restrained causes me to… quiver, *but is the quiver caused by fear or excitement?* I find myself lost in the idea, but also extremely nauseous.

In a low, intense, raspy voice Lance sneaks upon me and asks, "Is that what you want Lisa?"

"Crap, where did you come from?" I yelp.

G.L. Ross

"Is it, Lisa?" His voice is solemn, controlling, with an edge of tension and perhaps anger. *Maybe I shouldn't have used his computer.*

"Is it what?" I swivel the chair to face him. Our eyes meet and hold. We seem to be in some sort of stand-off. He demands an answer, from me. My voice strengthens before replying, "I don't know what I want. Is this what you want?" *At least I am honest.*

His eyes continue pushing me. He does his best to force me into a choice, an answer. A choice I've never even considered, much less vocalized. A deep guttural sound escapes my lips when I attempt an answer.

"Lisa?"

"I can't go there right now." I swear this is a battle of wills. *The question is am I battling myself or Lance?*

Lance pulls a chair beside me. His firm, tree trunk thigh brushes my knee. "Ask me."

Turbulent Passion

"Ask you what?" At least his voice is friendlier. I'm sure he was shocked to find me on his computer. I have no doubt in my mind I wasn't supposed to know about this…dark, kinky side Lance apparently has. *As I mentioned there are many shades comprising Lance.*

"Lisa, I know you have questions. Look at the photos and allow me to explain." His right hand laces and shrouds my left. *Is this what he expects of me?* Lance's palms are sweaty. His palms are never sweaty. Flyboy is nervous.

I dig deep to settle my voice and nerves before beginning. "She is being spanked. Do you enjoy being spanked or do you do the spanking? You are into all of this, right?"

Lance inhales deeply before answering. His grip tightens on my hand. "Yes, I enjoy some of these activities, but I would *never* ask you to do this." I should be relieved, *yet I feel…disappointed?* Lance continues in a staccato speech style, "I am not spanked. I do the spanking." Oh my, *did my sex just clench?"*

G.L. Ross

"What about the canes and whips?" *I know I won't go there.*

"I'm not a fan of leaving whelps, so I don't use those. I do enjoy restraints, floggers, and *many* toys."

"Floggers?" I ask. *Yes, I'm curious.*

"Yea, see the short, red, suede item in this picture?" Lance directs my attention to an item that is about the size of a feather duster, but with suede strips rather than feathers.

"I see. What do you do with it?"

"I would prefer to show you," he growls and grins. "But as far as a description, it would be dragged and slightly slapped against delectable parts of your body to heighten your sensations and pleasure." *I can't imagine my senses being heightened more than they were last night or this morning.*

I lick my lips and Lance moans, "You're killing me woman. Keep that tongue inside your

Turbulent Passion

mouth or else I am taking you to bed now and will demonstrate all these items."

I bite my bottom lip before continuing, "What about these outfits and toys?"

Lance's darkened eyes shoot me a coy look. "I enjoy many toys. There are vibrators, anal beads, butt plugs, nipple clamps, and so on." *Nipple clamps? Anal beads?* I'm not sure about this and I have a feeling my face reflects every single bit of my concern. "Lisa, I told you we don't need to go there. I'm happy with us. I am more than happy with us. I am in love with you." My heart leaps. *He is happy and he loves me. He doesn't have to have this – but does he want this?*

"I want you to stay happy. Obviously you enjoy this and if you don't get it from me you're gonna go somewhere else for it and I don't share, Lance."

"Baby, I'm not going anywhere, but right here." Lance lifts and slides me on to his lap. His fingers tip my chin. "You give me all I need, I promise." He places an imaginary cross on top of his heart. "I've never been this happy, Lisa. You are the absolute world to me. I will never ask you to give more than you are comfortable giving. Please know you have the power in this relationship. If you tell me 'no' then it's over."

My eyes lower as I embarrassingly admit, "Being a bad girl kind of excites me." My face is now turning several shades of red.

I sense Lance's smile before I actually see it. "Really? I don't want you to be uncomfortable, but I will gladly play with you." He kisses my cheek before continuing, "We can test your limits and explore your wild side, baby." His hand squeezes my backside.

I sternly state, "Okay, but no whips, chains, belts, canes, anything that leaves a mark."

"I have no desire to leave marks on your beautiful body, Goddess. Although, the restraints sometimes leave indentations, but they quickly subside."

"Restraints, Lance?"

Turbulent Passion

"We will start by using silk ties or velvet covered handcuffs." *Handcuffs, do I get to cuff him?*

I'm really not sure about using restraints, but I am willing to try for my prince. I certainly don't want him searching somewhere else for his "fun." I want *all* of Lance, *especially when it comes to between the sheets "fun."*

I suppress my growing fear as Lance's finger wisps a tendril of hair behind my ear. He whispers his wild, hungry desires for us to explore my "bad girl" side. His sexual explanations of what he wants to do to me and how he wants me to reciprocate send my body into orgasmic vibrations. This is our problem and blessing…we both are turned on by the raw hunger we emit when near each other's touch. We truly are addicted to each other. *We crave each other.*

"Come with me, Lisa." His eyes darken while his voice lowers into a raspy, sultriness. Panic begins to grow inside my chest. *Maybe I want to be a good girl after all.*

G.L. Ross

"So what happened to our drive?" I sheepishly ask.

"That was before."

Oh, my man is turned on. Everything about him is now wickedly dark and commanding. He's in control and devilishly handsome. I suppose he is the dominant that I have read about in novels, but, if so, that makes me the submissive. *I don't consider myself submissive.*

Electricity crackles and sizzles in the air. "Come here baby." Oh my, he *is* the dominant. His mannerisms and body language have altered completely. He is on fire and *damn sexy*. "Undress," he commands. *Okay, I'm salivating.*

"Lance, when did you and how did you become involved with BDSM?" I inquire. *When I'm nervous I talk.*

The feel of his hand caressing my nude backside is off the chart sensuous. I relish his heated

Turbulent Passion

touch until his hand smacks firmly against my ass. "No questions, Lisa. You speak when I ask you to speak." I flinch against his assault. Daunting eyes gaze down upon me. My eyes prickle, but I fight back my unshed tears. I defied his rules, *but I didn't know there were rules.* While I'm reeling and absorbing the pain inflicted on me by my *lover,* my dominant is kissing the imprint of his hand on my tender, red ass. My "Master" circles and assesses me, prior to removing two silk ties from his closet. Once again his voice alters and becomes a reassuring velvet caress for my heart and assaulted emotions. "It will be okay," he says as he leads me to a wing back chair in the corner of his bedroom.

Lance creates a silk tie slip knot around my left wrist. He repeats the action on my right side. My arms are pulled outside of the wing back chair. My Master pulls the silk ties to meet behind the chair and laces them together, causing my arms to pull and my chest to arch. It isn't painful, but there is definite tension in my arms and chest. I try to regulate my breathing. I am nervous, but I also find this very alluring. Lance returns to stand in front of me. The dark look and tone has returned.

"Lisa, I am in control in this bedroom." *Oh yes you are.* "You will not speak or cum until I tell you to. You will be ready and available whenever and however I desire you." A turbulent passion develops inside me. My body sizzles for his touch. I've never considered being controlled. I've never been interested in alpha male types, *until Lance.* Alpha's always turned my stomach. *So, why do I desire Lance's control?*

My masculine masterpiece kneels and spreads my knees. His black eyes initiate a shiver snaking its way through my body. Lance leans against a bookcase all predatory and irresistibly hot. His arms cross his chest and one of his ankles crosses the other. He reclines and admires his handiwork. The tension in my arms and the throbbing between my legs is causing me to feel weak and unsteady. *Maybe this wasn't a good idea after all. He was happy the way we were. I should stop him. Stop it now.*

Turbulent Passion

"Goddess, I am no boy scout or saint. You might as well accept that now, but *I love you*, so if things become too intense and you want me to stop you need to say, 'Flyboy.' Do you understand?" I nod my head. "No, Lisa. Speak," he orders abruptly.

"I understand." But – say, "But."

"What is the safe word?"

"Flyboy."

"Correct. Good girl."

Lance undresses in front of me, taunting me with his lengthy erection and wry smile. The man is sex-on-a-stick and boy do I want to lick him. My body yearns and aches for his touch. His magnetism is my aphrodisiac. *I can do this – for us.* Sex-on-a-stick crawls towards me with that continued predatory look in his eyes. He pushes my thighs further apart until the lips of my sex separate. My right foot is placed in his warm hand. He kisses his way up my inner thigh, teasing my sensitive skin

G.L. Ross

with his ticklish kisses. Once he reaches my pulsing sex he licks my desire and places my leg over the armrest. *Why do I have such an intense need for this man?*

Next, he places my other foot in his hand, but this time he licks his way up my inner thigh, before flicking his tongue across my throbbing clit. This erotic play has heightened every one of my senses. My head tips back as I release the loudest moan I've ever uttered. *I'm honestly embarrassed the noise came from me.* Lance tosses my leg over the armrest. Hiked up and spread out, in all my glory, Lance leans back to enjoy his raw view. "You are breathtakingly sexy my green-eyed Goddess. I have to taste all of you." I lift my head and see him reveling in his masculine triumphant state, of being completely in charge - *of me.*

A slick, white hot heat spreads between my thighs. *It is exhilarating being spread out, worshipped, and no longer in control.* I can't explain it. *You have to experience it for yourself.* My legs tremble from the burning touch of his fingertips stroking my thighs and abdomen. Pleasure pulsates

Turbulent Passion

through my body. I'm spread eagle in front of him and I don't care. I love his undivided attention and talented, experienced touch. *Consume me.* Please take all of me into your salacious mouth. A fiery storm brews in his eyes. With each teasing lick, he reminds me of how much he loves my taste. I'm trembling on the edge of another orgasm when Lance consumes my entire sex with the warmth of his mouth. His tongue sweeps across my cleft before spearing into me. I buck forward against his mouth as my arms ache to be freed. "Don't you cum. I want to eat all of you," he orders. "You will not cum until I tell you or else you will be punished."

"Oh please," I scream. I crave his control, but I want and need to cum. A sob slips from my lips. My legs begin to slide from the chair arms due to exhaustion and perspiration. Lance, the relentless lover he is, throws my legs over his shoulders and continues to circle my clit with his persistent tongue. With each swirl he presses his tongue against my bulging clit; the held pressure continues the reverberations through my sex. In my exhausted, limp state all I can do is lie there at his complete and

G.L. Ross

total mercy. After seeing the enjoyment on his face, I know we are far from finished.

"Lance, please," I beg through my choked voice. Maybe I should take the punishment. This seems like punishment to me.

"Hush. You do not mind. You, my Goddess, are a spitfire." He kisses his way across my stomach and then plumps and teases my hypersensitive nipples and breasts with his warm palms. My breasts are painfully full and heavy. Lance slides a hand under my hips pulling me towards the edge of the chair. My breathing becomes shallow and sporadically halts. *I must stop holding my breath.* My arms ache from the tightened constraint. Every one of my barriers is gone. I become disgustingly pliant. He commands me and I obey. I want him inside my body so badly I will do anything he demands. In one sweeping moment he thrusts himself completely into me. I arch and feel his heavy balls slap against me at the same time I feel his tip ramming against my sensitive inner wall. The mix of pain and pleasure rains upon my nerve endings. *He has claimed me.*

Turbulent Passion

"You are mine, Lisa, only mine. Say it," he screams.

He withdraws from me and I literally ache for his return. "Say it," he barks as he walks behind the chair.

"I am yours and only yours," I whimper. *Please* get back inside me, deep inside me.

The inner walls of my sex spasm and ache for his return.

My arms are released, but I am too weak to rub the soreness. Besides, the fully erect, heavy veined cock I crave stands pulsing and glistening from my juices in front of me. "Say it, so I believe it, Lisa."

"I am yours and only yours. But, are you only mine?" I scream and sob. Shock widens his eyes. In a flash, the shock switches to heat. I search for air while Lance lifts me and lowers us to the ground.

"Perhaps this will show you that I am only yours." Lance holds me above his beautifully chorded body and suspends my hips above his rock hard, throbbing erection. He pulls me down on to his

G.L. Ross

pulsing cock as he hammers his hips upward searing his heated sex into my aching arousal. Another orgasm rips violently through my body as I scream his name. I can't absorb its fierceness. Tears fall from my face as I ride his sex. "Baby, what's wrong," Lance asks while sitting up to face and hold me.

"Isn't it wrong to feel pleasure from pain? I mean, you feel incredible and instinctively you know my every need and meet it, even when I don't realize I need it. Part of this I really like, but it feels wrong."

Lance wraps his arms tightly around me and rolls so he is on top. "Lisa, you are all I need for the rest of my life. No one else gets me like you do. We were made for each other. We don't need these games or thrills. I want us, *but* two consenting adults playing roughly is not wrong."

"I want us too, Lance. Make love to me, but love me deep, hard, and recklessly. Let me try it your way."

"Gladly baby, but don't let me hurt you. I told you we don't have to play this way." I inhale deeply as Lance tilts my hips and repositions his

Turbulent Passion

thick crown before slamming into my depth. His moan is an animalistic roar and causes my entire body to shutter and tingle. Slowly he retreats before nailing me from his tip to his root, repetitively. Rising to his knees he lifts me pushing his thickening and lengthening cock deeper and faster. His abdomen and chest tighten and tremble as his hip and ass muscles jerk back and forth filling me with raw, pleasurable sensations. *I love what this man makes me feel.* His long fingers dig into my hips. His gorgeous face distorts from our wicked pleasure. My eyes are glued to his excitement and need as he punishes and pleasures my body. I feel the stretching of my sex as his width expands with his arousal. I am haunted by the excitement of our rough, sensual, sexual playing. *Maybe I am a bad girl? Perhaps this is the real me.* It feels good to have someone else in charge, someone who loves me and will protect me, someone I trust, while expanding my limitations.

Lances' body begins to jerk. His head falls back as he releases several guttural growls. It amazes and thrills me I have this effect on such a perfect masculine specimen. He craves me. He needs me. I

G.L. Ross

am his drug of choice. "Lisa, you are killing me," he screams as he releases his last shuddering expulsion inside me. *I can't help but smile.* Flyboy descends and lands on top of me drained and delighted.

I think I may have died and arrived in heaven *or perhaps hell*, with Lance pulsating deeply inside me.

Turbulent Passion

Chapter Seventeen

Monogamous

The last few weeks with the Goddess have been an actual "dream come true," even the week she had the flu. It was kind of nice delivering chicken soup to my sick baby. *Who would have thought?*

I need to tell Lisa about my Goddess dreams. I don't want her to freak out or think I'm a psycho stalker, but she needs to know.

Damn Your Eyes by Alex Clare is playing on my Ipod. The chorus in the song gets me every time: "Damn your eyes! They're taking my breath away. For making me wanna stay. Damn your eyes. For getting my hopes up high. Making me fall in love again. Damn your eyes!"

Lisa's eyes haunted me in my dreams for twenty plus years and they continue to permeate my life today. Being in love with Lisa is fantastic, but it's also scary as hell. I've never been in love, but every minute we spend together I fall deeper in love with Lisa. Quite honestly the thought of being with one woman, even with Lisa, scares the shit out of me.

G.L. Ross

Especially since she still hasn't reciprocated the words. I've put myself out there and if she dumps me I think I would totally lose it.

I've had many opportunities to be with other women on my overnights, but I've stayed monogamous. I am doing my very best to be a man worthy of Lisa. *A better Lance.* I know she loves me. *I simply wish she would say the words.*

Tonight I'm in Austin. Lisa is overnighting in Aspen. We try to fly the same days so when we are off we can spend time together. Really never thought I would plan my life around a woman's.

"Lance, are we changing and heading to 6th Street?" Jeff asks.

"Yea. How about in fifteen minutes we meet here, in the lobby?" Jeff is a nice guy. He is a good FO. But, man is he conservative. I have a feeling the ladies will devour him.

"Sounds good."

Turbulent Passion

"Ladies, are you gracing us with your presence tonight?" I flirtatiously inquire. I can't order from the menu, but I can damn sure read it!

Fortunately, for Jeff, the ladies agree to join us. *Let the festivities begin.*

Three hours later my crew and I tumble our way into the hotel lobby which connects with the bar. We have danced and partied our way across downtown Austin.

Jeff is in heaven enjoying the Los Angeles flight attendant crews' attention. The three ladies are all single and seeking both of us. Heaven is smiling on Jeff. *I am behaving.*

"You guys grab a table and I will get us a round of drinks," Jeff shouts. I have a girl under each of my arms and I must admit I have a fruitful, abundant view of some plastic surgeons handiwork. Jeff returns to our table with three beers and two red wines. "Hey, Lance. Isn't that Lisa over there?"

Without even checking to see I reply, "Nah, Lisa is in Aspen tonight." I continue to "read the menu" of my off limit arm candy.

G.L. Ross

"Lance, I am telling you that is Lisa and she is shooting daggers your way." My head turns to prove Jeff wrong, when I am blasted by the venomous green eyes of my Goddess. *Damn those eyes!*

Emotional

I am hyperventilating. The thought of Lance being with someone other than me is unnerving, but seeing him touch someone else is, well, it's heartbreaking. I have to get out of here. I stand to leave the bar, but, unfortunately, my knees wobble and give way. The torture of seeing Lance cheat on me is more than I am physically able to bear.

Lance rockets to his feet. *I have to get out of here.* He cuts me off as I make my way towards the hotel lobby. I do everything in my power to avoid his hypnotizing eyes. I can't stand to even look at him right now.

"Lisa! What the hell are you doing? Why are you here and running from me?"

Turbulent Passion

Lance is embarrassing the hell out of me. He is causing a major scene in the middle of the hotel lobby. Several crews are watching our domestic display. *Can't wait to hear how quickly this spreads through the gossip channels.*

"Don't scream at her. She isn't doing anything wrong - unlike you." Marie, a fellow flight attendant reprimands Lance. *Girl Power!*

"Don't tell me how to talk to my woman." Lance and Marie actively participate in a shouting exchange while I search the bar for help. Finally three pilots jump up and intervene. As they diffuse Lance and Marie's temper tantrums I escape to the elevators.

Why? Why God? I thought we were secure. I thought we were happy. He said I was his "everything." *But, does anyone really know the depth of Lance's feelings...regarding anything?* And he wonders why I am afraid to say those three special words.

I lock and chain my hotel room door once safely inside. *I will not cry!* I change into my white,

G.L. Ross

short, silky robe and lace panties. Since I've been sleeping with Lance, I have grown accustom to sleeping in nothing, but since there could be an emergency I sleep in panties and keep a robe nearby when at work.

Nervously I channel surf after crawling into bed. I have no idea what is on the screen. My mind keeps replaying Lance's hungry gaze as he huddled with the bosom buddies. To hell with the TV, I turn it off and plug in my Ipod. Lance's song, *Damn Your Eyes,* begins to play. He likes the cover by Alex Clare. I like Alex, but I prefer the classic Etta James version. Lance loves the music and its' lyrics, but right now certain lyrics are speaking to *me*, "You say that you'll change. Somehow you never do. I believe all your lies. The look in your eyes….With that look I know so well, I fall completely under your spell." *Yep, that about sums it up.* I knew he couldn't be faithful. I knew I couldn't fill that dark void he harbors. But, I fell under his spell - *Damn it!*

"Open the door, Lisa," Lance shouts while creating *another* unwelcome scene, but this time in the hallway outside my door. *I could let security take*

Turbulent Passion

him away, but then he would get in trouble with the company. "I mean it, Lisa. I will kick the damn door in!" *Shit!* I don't want to deal with him, especially like this, but I don't want everyone else disturbed. One never knows when Lance's gentleness will turn dark. He is pissed, but Lance would never physically hurt me ... emotionally... well, that's a completely separate issue.

He is ramming the damn door. WTH? I have to answer…God, help me, please.

I fling the door open and glare at the cheating son of a bitch standing in front of me. "Lance, stop it! Get in here and shut up." *Be strong, Lisa!*

His eyes are frightening. Each pupil is close to filling each eye. His jaw is clenched and his hands are fisted. He stands so close I hear his chest rumbling with tension. Our hurt-filled eyes lock and Lance reacts by slamming his fist into the wall beside my head.

I scream at my over the top alpha-male, "Damn it, Lance. Stop!" He cages me with his palms

G.L. Ross

planted firmly against the wall. *Trapped.* My eyes shoot daggers into his. His predatory instincts have taken hold and I am his prey. I should attempt to escape, but instead I hear a voice inside my head saying, "Take me. Please, take all of me." Immediately another voice pops up, "I thought you loved me. I thought we were the real deal." *Who should I listen to?*

Lance realizes he is frightening me. His voice alters into a husky, tension-filled decrescendo. Softly he asks, "Why are you in Austin? Were you rerouted? Why didn't you call? You knew I was here." *Give me a chance to answer!*

I am desperate to escape his torturous trap, but at the same time this gorgeous, hot blooded man is tempting me and as usual arousal strikes my core. *Why...How does he always do this to me?*

"I was rerouted, Lance. Something I am sure you have heard of," I snap.

In a low grumble he replies, "That doesn't explain you not telling me."

Turbulent Passion

I raise my eyes to lock with his before answering. "I was waiting in the bar for you to return. I wanted to surprise you. I wasn't about to leave the hotel in Austin, not after everything that happened before and I figured you were eating dinner with your crew. Of course, when you came in drooling over the heaving chests of two of our finest I decided to leave." I dip under his arm and walk across the room.

Lance paces the room resembling a caged animal. His hands slide in and out of his hair, before he finally erupts. "I screwed up, by flirting. I know it. Lisa you scare the hell out of me, but I would never cheat on you. I can read the menu. Can't I? I didn't order from it." *What?*

With hands on my hips I blurt, "And you think I'm not scared?"

"Why would you be scared? You're the one in control. Shit, you have me by my damn balls, Lisa. I can't think without you taking over my thoughts."

"Obviously your thoughts were elsewhere when they led your eyes to the bosoms of your *buddies*." I turn my back to him. I need to think

G.L. Ross

rationally, which is impossible when looking at Captain America and his mesmerizing baby blues.

His voice lowers becoming softly sincere, "They are nothing to me. Lisa – jeez Lisa, you are *everything* to me and it overwhelms me. I've never cared or worried about anyone, except myself. I've never allowed someone else to control me in any way, shape, or form, but you do." My heart aches for the little boy inside Lance who desperately tries to be good, but keeps misbehaving. *Lance wants to be loved, unconditionally. I want to trust and love him, unconditionally. I really do.* But, why should I have to be around for him to behave?

"I don't try to control you," I calmly explain while taking a few steps towards him.

Annoyed Lance snaps, "I know. I know you don't." My eyes display my shock regarding his tone. His voice softens once again before continuing, "I know, but you do. Lisa, I could never be with those girls. No one measures up to you, baby." Lance cups my face with his warm hands. The fevered intensity in his eyes causes me to tremble. "You are my Goddess. You, baby, only you."

Turbulent Passion

"You have an odd way of showing it."

"Lisa, I think of you and I smile. I look at you and I ache. I hold you and I find myself willing to give up everything in the world to protect you. It will always be you for me."

I admonish him, "I don't need you to protect me."

"Fine, but I want to. For the first time in my life, I want to put someone else's needs before mine." Lance kisses the tip of my nose, before pressing his lips to mine.

Against his lips I ask, "Are you sure I can give you what you need?"

"What the hell are you talking about? You do. You give me more than I deserve." His hands slide down my hair before resting on my shoulders. "I don't deserve you, but I fucking need you. Lisa, give us a chance. I will work every day to earn your love and trust." His eyes fill with tears. "I may look at those women, but they are not my future. Baby, tell me how you see our future." His hands slide down the front of my robe's lapel to untie the belt. His

G.L. Ross

hands melt and became one with my hip bones. Lance can never be close enough, even when inside me. He wants to possess all of me, *his Goddess.*

The silky robe puddles in the floor. Lance's fingertips mark the cheeks of my ass as he lifts me against his erection. *Did he ask me a question? I think he did, but my mind is all foggy.* I search flyboys' steamy eyes. His fingers slide through my hot and heavy arousal. With a moan, he closes his eyes and I surrender my fears.

Lance's eyes slowly open. His voice is now low and authoritative. His demeanor has changed. "No one else will ever have you. Do you hear me?" My dominant is back and I'm ready, willing, and able. "I will fuck you so hard and so long you will never want to think of another man." *Yes, please.* "Hell, you will be so delirious you won't even remember your own name much less anyone else's." He wants to own me; then own me. I should fight him, but why? *He already owns me, doesn't he?*

My excitement has wet the way for his erection to slide easily inside me. The sensation of him playing with my hypersensitive bulging button is

Turbulent Passion

driving me up and over the edge of reason. "Get inside me now." He spurts his pre-cum against my opening, teasing me with his tip. "Damn it, Lance, get inside me." He lifts and lowers me onto his lengthy erection. His sizzling heat radiates into my eyes and between my thighs. He proceeds to slam through me like a red hot fire poker. Fire ignites within my core pulsing and squeezing him tight. He shudders and pumps into me pulling me against him so I am able to experience the friction our bodies create together. Circling his hips he pushes me against the room's wall driving me into a frenzied state. Rubbing against each other we squeeze out the remnants of our orgasms. My wrists are above my head as he pushes me up and over another ledge before collapsing against me.

Our bodies continue to slide against each other craving skin against skin contact. I whisper against his ear, "I will do my best to please you always. I want to make you happy, Lance. I want you to feel as good as you make me feel." My fingers continue to play with the hair brushing the nape of his neck.

G.L. Ross

His lips slide briefly across mine. "I love you. Please believe me. You make me happier than I've ever been or imagined. You are my world, Lisa. You are the air I breathe. I would suffocate and die without you. I belong to you….do you get that? Please tell me you get that."

Lance carries me to the bed curling on his side to face me. He tenderly embraces my face. While staring into my eyes he whispers against my lips, "You are mine and I am yours, only yours." His voice is thick with emotion. "Your mind needs to be full of us, happily together, always."

He continues holding my face kissing and urging me to respond to his touch, to his love. The sexual tension between us is combustible. I turn away from him to think. He spoons his body against mine. He speaks before placing a kiss on my ear, "I will protect and love you, always. I will never cheat on you, Lisa."

"Can you protect my heart?" I ask as a tear trickles down my cheek. My feelings and intense love for Lance frightens me and for some stupid reason I am an emotional crybaby.

Turbulent Passion

"I can protect all of you if you let me. I love you. I've never said those words to anyone else and I never will." He kisses the back of my head.

With Lance, I always feel loved, treasured, and cared for; I feel safe and am able to give myself completely. I trust him or at least I was learning to, until tonight. *Lisa, you know you trust him. He would not have cheated and you know that in your heart.* I love and crave Lance, but I will not be controlled by a man or my cravings. It isn't healthy to lose yourself in someone.

The thing is I feel as though I finally found Lisa when I found Lance.

****

I have to admit it is nice to be back at the airport, especially after being off an entire week due to a nasty stomach virus. *Everything I ate made me ill.*

There's an excitement about traveling and the ability to leave all stress and cares behind. One of the many great things about being a flight attendant is that once you get off your trip you are done. There's

G.L. Ross

no paperwork to file or phone calls to return. Today I'm looking forward to serving my passengers and spoiling myself with room service and a hot bubble bath. First, I deserve a treat, a latte, before reporting to my gate. "Hi, may I have an extra hot pumpkin spice latte?"

"Whipped topping, mam?" The clerk is busy writing my order on the cup.

"Sure, why not?" I earned the whip cream after all my work outs, *with Lance.*

I pay the clerk placing the change in my coin purse. "Thanks mam, your latte may be picked up at the end of the counter. Have a safe flight."

"You have a great day…" What does her name tag say? I try to use people's first names when possible. It seems friendlier. "…Kate." Better grab a sleeve, so I can hold the extra hot latte.

"Pumpkin Spice latte, extra hot with whip, for Lisa." I approach the counter and claim my scrumptious treat. I better grab some napkins too, just in case.

Turbulent Passion

"Thanks Kate." When I turn around I bump smack into Ken, a Captain at International Air. Ken is around 6'4", built, tan, and I think about ten years older than me.

"Lisa, hello and thank you for making my day." He is such a flirt and tries his best to sound suave. *Which he doesn't.*

I quickly try to balance the hot coffee cup. "Ha, hello Ken. You are very lucky you are not wearing this coffee or I definitely would *not* be making your day." *Glad I grabbed a few napkins.*

"Touché Lisa, so very true, but it was nice being able to grab your shoulders." Ken is really handsome and in some ways charming, but he is such a player or at least that's his reputation. He's always been a gentleman around me, but as Steve Harvey says, "the lady must let her limits and expectations be known upfront" and I have heeded his advice.

"So where are you off to, Ken?"

"Kansas City tonight, Milwaukee tomorrow. How about you?"

G.L. Ross

"I think I'm with you - that sounds like my trip. This is a four day trip, which I despise, but at least I have a good crew." I pull my trip sheet from my pocket. "Do you go to Oklahoma City first?"

My goodness Ken has a smile from ear to ear. "Yes mam."

I give up. What is this mam thing? I guess I am a *mam*; first Stephen, then latte gal, and now Ken. "Then it looks as though we are together for the next few days."

Ken extends his arm to me, "Well Lisa, may I escort you to the gate?" *Oh my, gate check*, but, hey I'm with the Captain. *The plane can't leave without him.* Today is going to be a good day. *I just feel it.*

I decide to spend a few minutes checking for a trade on the gate computer before heading down the jetway. A message pops up, "We need to talk. If you have time on your overnight please give me a call. Saw you are flying with Ken tell him to behave ☺ Have fun Lisa, just not too much fun - unless of course you are with me. xoxo, Lance."

Turbulent Passion

That man even seduces me via an email. How does he do that?

"Hey girlie. What or should I say who has put that smile on your face?" I lift my head and find my dear sweet friend, Nick, standing next to me.

I eagerly jump to my feet and wrap him in a huge hug. "Nick, so happy to see you! You going out on a trip?"

"I was just assigned to your trip. Your mid-cabin flight attendant called in sick, so you have three days to explain that smile on your face. I have a feeling his name is spelled L-A-N-C-E." This trip just keeps getting better and better. *Have I mentioned I love my job?*

"Guilty as charged. I will give you all the details once on the plane, but right now I need to return an email." Nick is giving me a raised eyebrow and a cocked head. "On the plane, Nick."

"Fine." Nick struts off to flirt with the many female flight attendants and customer service agents looking his way. He is such a cutie.

G.L. Ross

I need to respond to Lance, but what to say? *Start typing girl.*

"Dear Lance, as far as having too much fun - I believe that is a definite possibility. Breathe Lance; ☺ Nick has been assigned to my trip. Ken is very nice on the eyes, but not really my type. I prefer alpha-males with huge egos. I have to run. Promise to call, Lisa." I know I love him, but I want to tell him in person. It's the right thing to do, *for both of us.* I need to feel his arms around me after I say those three special words.

Alright, time to put Lance in the back of my mind and get to work, on the plane. Now, where is Nick?

I turn the corner and there is Mr. Cutie himself flirting with the ladies, of course. *What a mess that man is.* "Nick, come on we have three minutes to get on the plane. Sorry ladies…I have to take him."

"Bye Nick." *Jeez, it sounds like a soprano chorus.* He does have a way with the ladies.

Turbulent Passion

Within my purse, I hear my phone beep with a text message. I decide to check it once on the plane, since I am already cutting it close on time. Nick and I board the plane and head to the aft galley. "Glad you are working in the back with me, Nick." Nick hoists my roller bag into the overhead bin. *There are definite perks to flying with "boy stews."* "Wish your jump seat was back here, so we could have 'jump seat confessions.'" I laugh and smile endearingly at my dear, sweet friend.

"Me too, but I must admit Carol is a great forward flight attendant. Trust me I will have her confessing to me before the day is done."

"Oh, I have no doubt you charmer, you. Carol is a terrific flight attendant. If I were ever in an emergency I would want her with me. Thank goodness the only emergency I've ever had is a button pushed for either emergency trash or an emergency drink."

"Lisa you always crack me up. Go log in the liquor and I will check the equipment."

G.L. Ross

"Thanks Nick." First, I need to see who texted me. Where is my phone? I put way too much in my purse when flying. I can never find anything in here. Wait, I think I see it; there it is under my make-up bag. Two texts from – Lance. *The man is persistent.*

The message reads, "Lisa, I forgot to ask you to say hello to Nick for me. I know he will take good care of you. Perhaps I should call him to make sure you do not have too much fun without me…xo, your loving alpha male with a humongous ego, Lance." Oh my gracious, *he does love me.*

After a day of turbulence I am so happy to finally be in Kansas City. Since I am once again nauseous; I am glad to finally be on the ground and at the hotel. I'm really tired of not feeling well.

I love the beds at this hotel. Hopefully I will get a king-size bed that I can crawl in the middle of, with my room service tray. *Spoiled, yes that is me and I deserve it.*

Ken and Nick headed downstairs to drink and watch a ball game, but I opted for a bubble bath

Turbulent Passion

and a Sprite, to settle my stomach. Nick has promised to check on me before retiring to his room. Carol also decided to forego downstairs activities and went to her room, but to call her husband. The first officer lives here so he headed home for the night. All are accounted for and happy. *Life is good.* After my bath, I will call Lance.

I love the smell of my vanilla bean bubble bath. Sinking into the hot water and disappearing behind the bubbles is bliss, absolute bliss. *I so deserve this.* Think how wonderful this would be if Lance were here to join me. *I can't help but smile from ear to ear when I think of my chiseled masterpiece of a man.* I do love him.

After the third ring Lance answers his phone, "Hey Goddess, I miss you like crazy. You and Nick having a good time together?"

"Hey baby, I miss you too. Nick and Ken are downstairs playing, but Carol and I chose to stay in our rooms. So see, I am behaving," I purr.

"I so wish I were there to make you misbehave." *Okay, I'm wet.*

G.L. Ross

"Lance, I always misbehave with you – willingly. You don't have to make me do anything. I wish we had the same overnights. I miss you."

"Baby you are killing me. Do you know what I would like to do with you right now?" he asks in a whiskey-rough voice.

I return his raspy roughness with my purring, "No, but please share…"

Several hours later I am curled up in the middle of my cozy king-size bed still smiling. *Who knew phone sex could be so fun.*

There is another beep. Lance has to stop texting. I have to get some rest. Oh, not Lance, rather it's Nick. He's on his way up. I better grab my robe before I shock the boy. *LOL.*

"Hey Nicky, did you have fun?" I return to my propped pillows after opening the door. "Did you happen to remember the saltines?"

"Yes, I did. I also brought you a couple of other items. I hope you won't mind."

Turbulent Passion

"Why would I mind, Nick?" I un-wrap a cracker and begin chewing small, salty bites.

"Lisa, how long have you been fighting this nausea?" Nick sits close beside me on the bed while holding a brown paper bag.

"A few weeks, ever since I caught that yucky stomach virus. Why Nick?" Nick hands me a bottle of Sprite which I quickly pour into a glass. "It seems saltines and Sprite are the only items my stomach allows.

"Did you order soup from room service?" Nick kindly inquires.

"Yes, I drank the broth from the chicken noodle soup. They put more chicken in their soup than I care for personally, but it was good."

"Good, I'm glad you were able to keep something down, besides Sprite and crackers. Baby girl, is there any chance you could be pregnant?"

"What?" I ask in shock. "No! Gracious no, Nick," I adamantly deny.

G.L. Ross

"Lisa, think. When was your last period? The nausea. Perhaps you didn't have a virus, maybe it was morning sickness." Nick timidly pulls a pregnancy test from the brown bag. "It wouldn't hurt to take a test."

"Nick, I can't be," I choke over a half-chewed cracker. I gulp some Sprite and begin counting in my head. Oh my goodness. Could I be pregnant?" The room begins to spin.

"Lisa, you are as white as this sheet. I'll grab you a wet washcloth." Nick hurries to the bathroom for a cloth. "Here, baby girl." He places the cool, wet cloth across my forehead. "If you are pregnant it will be okay. Lance loves you." I run to the bathroom and heave into the toilet. Nick hurries after me and holds my hair as I continue to hurl. Tears flow as I face reality. "Don't cry Lisa. Take the test in the morning. Don't panic or worry until you know for sure." My true-blue friend consoles me until I finally fall fast asleep.

****

Turbulent Passion

Ready to attack the day in his crisp and pristine uniform, Nick cheerfully, yet hesitantly, greets me, "Good morning Lisa." *His statement sounds curiously like a question.*

I, on the other hand, pull my bag into the hotel lobby and flop into a nearby chair. "Is it a good morning? This is entirely too early for a PM trip and you are way too chipper Nick."

"This latte will make everything better or would you prefer a Sprite? I came prepared with both." Nick hands me my choice of beverages, with his beautiful smile, and an unspoken question served on the side.

"Thanks Nicky, not sure it will make *everything* better but it will definitely improve my attitude." I stand and give my fabulous friend a big hug for his kindness last night and today. "We are to report at 11:30, right?"

"Yea, the hotel clerk said the van should be here any minute. Carol and the guys are outside waiting for the van. She said she needed the cool air to wake her."

G.L. Ross

"I understand her pain," I mumble as I continue to sip my carbonated beverage.

"There's the van. Lisa, is everything okay?" Nick and I push through the revolving doors into the brisk Kansas City air.

"We will find out soon enough," I reply.

"Good morning Lisa. May I hold your coffee while you climb in the van?" Ken is obviously a morning person.

"Thank you, Ken. It seems I am always meeting you over coffee." I hand Ken my cup and climb inside the warm van. Why I am even attempting to balance two beverages is beyond me. I doubt my stomach will allow me to drink the latte, but Nick was extremely sweet to get it for me.

Ken openly flirts, "Well, meeting you over coffee is a great way to start my mornings." He is such a charmer *or should I say bull-shitter?* Bull-shitter it is.

Turbulent Passion

No wonder the girls call him the "panty dropper." Supposedly he can charm the panties off any girl he chooses, except of course "moi."

"Thank you Ken, as always so charming," I condescendingly respond. I choose a seat in the back of the van near an air condition vent. I seriously need to wake up, get control, *and stop being such a beeaatch. Where are the barf bags located on this mode of transportation?*

"My pleasure," Ken responds while handing me my "wake up" brew. Now I really feel like a bitch. He is being genuinely nice.

Nick has had enough of our bantering. "Break up the mutual admiration society and let the rest of us get in the van."

"Nick, I think you need more coffee," Ken antagonizingly jokes.

"No Ken, I think too much coffee is his problem," I jest. We all laugh as Nick heads to the back of the van to join me.

G.L. Ross

I'm reaching for my seat belt when Carol boards the van. "Hey Carol, is our first flight to Baltimore?"

"Yes, then to St Louis and on to Milwaukee." Carol sits in front of me and I hand her a seat belt shoulder strap.

"Thanks, Lisa. Now tonight the whole crew is going down for a crew 'debrief,' at the bar, right?"

"Absolutely," replies the chorus of crew members. *I love my job.*

"Ladies and Gentleman this is your Captain, Ken Martin, welcome aboard flight 422 service to Baltimore, Maryland. The skies are clear and it is a brisk forty-two degrees in Baltimore. You have three of the best flight attendants in the industry serving you today. Please let one of them know if we can make your experience more enjoyable. Once we get closer I will update you with more information. Thank you for choosing International Air."

Nick corners me in the back galley. "So? Are you?"

Turbulent Passion

"I haven't looked. I can't."

"What? You took the test, right?" Nick appears so confused. *Bless his heart.*

I attempt to explain my actions. "Yes, I took the test, but I haven't checked the results. I wanted to wait for you. I need you with me when I look." Tears, once again, pool in my eyes. *I despise being hormonal and emotional.*

"No tears baby girl. We will do it together and you will be able to handle the results, no matter what. I will help you." I wrap my arms tightly around Nick's waist placing my cheek against his chest. His gentle hand strokes my hair. "Get the stick, Lisa." We both laugh at his instruction and lack of tact.

I reach for my bag, but halt when I hear Carol's voice, "Ladies and gentlemen we have closed the front door of the aircraft, so at this time we need all portable electronic devices completely powered off or placed in airplane mode." Why is it passengers have such a difficult time letting go of their electronics? My parents didn't even have cell phones, they had to depend on pay phones, and they survived.

G.L. Ross

Making my way to mid-cabin, for the emergency demo, I encounter a "rule breaker." "Sir, are you powering down your phone?"

"Yes, mam." *I give up.* I think I'm getting used to being a mam.

In all honesty, I swear I have done this emergency demo so many times I don't even listen to the speech. I must go into auto-pilot mode. I seem to move through every motion and "zone out." Today, without a doubt, my mind is elsewhere.

I'm very blessed to have a great crew and to have a job I thoroughly enjoy. *Thank you, Lord.* Sometimes I think we forget to say thanks as often as we should.

As soon as we are airborne I begin to take my drink orders. Sometimes taking drink orders can be as difficult as managing Congress or as painful as pulling teeth. "What may I get you to drink sir?"

I look up from my drink order tablet as he replies, "Coke please."

Turbulent Passion

"Coke it is." I scribble a "C" on my pad. "Mam, what may I get you to drink?"

"I would like rum and pineapple juice, with a side of water." *Wrong airline sweetie.*

"I'm sorry mam, but we don't offer pineapple juice."

"Coconut water?" *Really?*

"No mam." I motion towards her seatback pocket. "There is a menu in your seatback pocket that lists all of our beverages."

"Oh, let me see… let's change it to a vodka cranberry, with a side of water."

"Yes mam, vodka/cranberry, with a side of water. Would you care for a lime in the cocktail?"

"That would be very nice. Only a couple of cubes of ice in the water." *I swear there is at least one in every group*, the ultimate in high maintenance. Pineapple juice, coconut water, and two cubes of ice, she has to be from California. Can't wait to get to the galley and tell Nick this one.

G.L. Ross

"Excuse me, Nick, would you pass me the pineapple juice and coconut water?"

While turning to the juice drawer, it dawns on Nick what I have said. "Sure - uh, what? Did you say pineapple juice and coconut water?" Nick's reaction is hilarious. I burst into giggles.

Nick spouts off, "It's with my green tea fruit smoothie and pressed wheat grass."

"Exactly." My eyes sparkle with humor. "Pressed wheat grass - that's a good one, Nick."

"Thank you Lisa. California transplant?"

"Has to be. She even wants a side of water." I start pulling out supplies preparing for my service.

"Well I have five hot chocolates, all for kids. What part of burning flesh in turbulence do parents not understand?"

"I agree. Apple juice sounds like the best choice for kiddos."

"Was that a call button?" Nick looks up the aisle.

Turbulent Passion

"I'll get it Nick. You find the coconut water." I laugh as I head to mid-cabin where the emergency flight attendant call button's lit. It had better not be emergency trash again. "Yes mam, may I help you?"

The middle-aged woman is pointing out the window. "Yes, sweetie could you tell me what lake that is down there?"

Is she serious? I swear they think we are tour guides and meteorologists. I press the light to reset her flight attendant call button allowing me time to count to ten before answering. "Mam, I never have an opportunity to look out the window, so I'm afraid I have no idea. But, I will be happy to ring the Captain and see if I can find an answer for you."

"That would be wonderful." Flashing my "friendly" smile I return to the aft galley. Ken is going to love this. I'm sure he'll have the rookie first officer be the tour guide and meteorologist. Rookie initiation, they get all the grunt work.

G.L. Ross

I ring the cockpit and wait for their answer. "This is Captain Ken ready and willing to serve, unless this is Nick."

I bust a gut for several seconds before I'm able to form a sentence. "Ken that was a good one."

"Glad I could brighten your day, Miss Lisa. Now, what may I really do for you? Want to come visit us?"

"So sorry, far too busy with this high maintenance group. I'm calling for your tour guide expertise."

"Let me guess - what city is down there?"

"Even better - what is the lake we just passed?"

"Well - there wasn't a lake, but we did cross the Mississippi River."

"Will you make an announcement?" I request.

"Sure, anything for you Lisa." Even his voice sounds as though he would love to undress me.

Turbulent Passion

•

"You really are such the sweet talker, Ken." I hang up the phone and return to prepare my drinks.

Nick chimes in, "So, what was all that and *when* are you going to *get that stick?*"

"After the customers are taken care of *and* that was about tour guide services."

"Do we charge for that?"

"OMG. You are on a roll." I snort, *actually snort*, and it feels so good to laugh and let go.

Prior to exiting the galley to serve his drinks, Nick replies, "I figure if a bag is fifty then tour guide services should be at least seventy five dollars."

"Nick, I love flying with you," I shout after him. *I must find him a good southern girl.*

The first officer, *as I predicted*, comes on the speaker explaining how we recently crossed the Mississippi River. He even gives geographical information regarding where the river begins and ends. I bet he loved geography in high school.

G.L. Ross

Anyway, back to the drinks. *Two ice cubes in Miss California's water.*

Nick inquisitively turns the corner. "Lisa, did he cut that announcement off?"

"What do you mean?" I'm still trying to decipher my scribbled tablet orders.

"I swear he stopped mid-sentence."

I continue mixing my cocktails. "The tower probably interrupted him. I tune them out when they give tours and weather reports. Plus, it's too loud back here to hear them half the time."

Out of nowhere the plane makes a sudden dip knocking Nick and me around the galley. Ken comes on the speaker instructing, "Flight Attendants take your seats, immediately."

"He doesn't have to tell me twice. Lisa, get over here." Nick immediately straps into his jump seat harness.

"I am trying. The trash can is in my way. The drop caused it to slide out." Carefully I push the

Turbulent Passion

can back into its slot and latch its door. Strapping in beside Nick, we cautiously wait for further information. Looking forward, I see Carol in the cabin carefully making her way to the forward jump seat. "Nick, that didn't feel like turbulence to me," I share while gingerly rubbing my hand across my belly.

"I didn't want to say anything but I thought it was weird, too." Nick and I continue to discuss the oddness of the situation, until the sound a flight attendant never wants to hear rings throughout the cabin - *five bells,* an emergency call from the cockpit.

I nervously grab the interphone to receive emergency instructions. "Captain this is Lisa. Nick and I are in the back."

"This is Carol in the front."

"Alright crew, we've lost our left engine and have ten minutes to prepare the cabin for an emergency landing in Chicago. Everyone set their watches for 12:48. I need all of you in your seats at 12:55. I'm not going to sugar coat this it's going to

G.L. Ross

be a major impact, so make sure the passengers are in their brace positions. Prepare now, 12:55 call me."

"Yes sir," we respond.

I grab Carol's attention before she disconnects. "Carol, are you there?"

"Yes Lisa."

"Nick and I will head to our demonstration positions. Grab your emergency preparedness form and let's get the brace positions explained first." In training, the instructors drilled this information into our minds, praying we would never have to use it, but knowing it would come to us even when scared "shitless." *They were correct.*

"I agree Lisa." The adrenaline shooting through my body is unlike any feeling or emotion I've ever known. Nick is staring at me with wide vacant eyes. As quickly as possible I explain to him what the Captain instructed. He stands frozen. *He's in shock.* I begin pushing him towards the front of the cabin.

Turbulent Passion

Carol begins to explain to the passengers what is happening, "Ladies and gentleman we are about to experience an emergency landing in Chicago. Please pay attention as the flight attendants explain and demonstrate the brace position for landing." I make eye contact with Nick urging him to remain calm and to do what he has been trained to do. "Please stay off of your cell phones and pay attention." As we explain the brace position and walk through the cabin, I hear people crying and calling their loved ones. I understand their desire to call, but at the same time this brace position may be the difference in life and death. I also check to see if there are any lap children in my section. Thank goodness the only infant is in a car seat; *money well spent*. Carol reminds everyone where the eight emergency exits are located. Time to check my watch - 12:52. Three minutes to secure my galley and take my seat.

I'm latching my galley compartments when I feel Nick's arms sliding around my waist. He tenderly kisses the back of my head. Resting his chin on my shoulder he softly says, "Lisa, I love you." He chokes back fear and tears before continuing, "If I don't survive please tell my parents how much I appreciate and love them."

Tears have gathered in Nick's eyes when I turn around to hug him. "Nick, we are going to make it." I fight back my own tears. *Damn hormones.* I sternly grab his shoulders and instruct him, "You say your prayers and get to that front jump seat. We will have a drink tonight to celebrate living." I force my "friendly smile" doing my very best to calm and encourage him.

"Always the optimist Lisa, I do love you. You will be a great mom." Nick's trembling chin rips my heart.

"But, I haven't…" Nick flashes me a half-hearted grin before turning to head to the front galley.

I start strapping into my jump seat, but then I decide it's time. It's time to face *every* single reality about to slap me in the face. I reach for the stick and shove it quickly into my apron, before strapping tightly into my jump seat.

Turbulent Passion

It's 12:55, I grab the interphone. Carol is already connected and talking to Ken. "Are you all seated and strapped in?"

"Yes sir," we reply.

"In two minutes we will make impact." Passengers begin to scream. I lean, to my right, in order to see up the aisle. Passengers are yelling about fire on the wing.

I interject, "Ken the right engine is on fire!"

Composed Ken firmly states, "Prepare for landing. Brace positions."

G.L. Ross

Turbulent Passion

Chapter Eighteen

Turbulent

"You're taking my plane?" *Are you fuckin' kidding me?* "So, when will my plane be here?" *Yes, I am pissed.* I didn't sleep well last night. All I can think about is Lisa, *my Lisa.* She is supposed to be on the ground in two hours, but now I will be in the air when she lands. *Can this day get any worse?*

"So Lance, what's the deal?" My FO asks.

"The deal is we are being screwed, by the *big picture,* again." Whenever scheduling messes with us and we offer a different suggestion or idea they tell us we don't see the "big picture." "We're here, in Chicago, for at least two hours until our plane arrives."

This is exactly what I needed more time to think about how much I miss my Goddess. *NOT!*

All morning I've felt off. I have this gut feeling of "gloom and doom," probably because I desperately miss the best thing to ever happen to me.

G.L. Ross

"You guys leave your bags here. I'll watch them. Go get food."

"Want us to get you something?" One of the flight attendants thoughtfully offers.

"Yea, a plane and my girl," I mumble while checking my phone for any messages from Lisa. Realistically I know there won't be any, she is in the air, but I still look. I know - I'm torturing myself.

Passion

I'm beyond frightened. We are descending too quickly. Ken is monumentally struggling to keep the plane level. The plane continues to bank. I know the guys are fighting to pull us even. Ken is a great Captain. *We will be fine.*

The sound of people screaming and crying is deafening. It's against the rules but I have to call him. I have to let him know the truth. I need to hear his voice. *In case...*

On the second ring, Lance answers his phone. "Baby, I'm so glad you called. I miss you."

Turbulent Passion

"Lance, hush and listen to me. I only have a minute." My nerves get the best of me. I begin squeezing my apron. *Anything to grab. Anything to hold.* Then I feel the stick and decide to face the inevitable. *It's time Lisa – look.*

"Lisa, what's wrong? I can hear that something is majorly wrong, in your voice."

Joy fills my heart as I stare at the stick. Then with a tip of the plane reality steals my joy. "My plane is doing an emergency landing in Chicago. I need you to listen to me." I fight to keep my voice steady. I can barely hear Carol and Nick shouting the commands, "Brace, Prepare, Brace." I need to join them, but I have to tell Lance. *I must be honest, with him.*

"I'm here in Chicago, baby. It's going to be okay. You are going to be okay. What's wrong with the plane?" *In his arms, I want to be wrapped in Lance's safe, protective arms. I don't want to be here.*

G.L. Ross

"Lance, please listen to me. The engine is on fire and it doesn't look good." I can no longer prevent the trembling in my voice no matter how hard I try.

"I'm walking onto the tarmac, baby. The fire trucks are on their way to the strip. It will be okay. Lisa I'm here to catch you, just like I said I always would. Smile my sweet Goddess; everything is going to be okay. I promise."

"Lance, listen to me, I love you. I had to tell you the truth, in case." I inhale deeply still staring at the stick in my hand.

"Oh baby, I love you. I know you love me. I've always known. We belong to each other. You belong to me, always. You are going to be okay. You hear me?"

"I wanted you to know. I can't let things end without you knowing the truth and hearing me say it. I love you, Lance Miller."

"Things aren't ending Lisa. They are just beginning, for us."

Turbulent Passion

"Lance, I don't – I don't think the plane's going to make it." I begin to chant sporadically, "Brace, Prepare, Brace."

"You listen to me! You will be fine," he howls over the roar of the runway noise.

"Lance, tell my parents I love them." My voice cracks as I yell, "Brace, Prepare, Brace."

"Lisa, stop this nonsense. You're going to be fine." Lance is firm, but I hear how tense and frightened he really is. I scream as the plane tips and vibrates.

Lance shouts, "Lisa, marry me!"

"What?"

"Marry me, Lisa."

"Lance don't. I love you. I wanted you to know the truth and there's something else."

Lance interrupts me, "Marry me, have my babies, grow old with me."

G.L. Ross

"Lance, only you could make me smile and laugh when I'm about to die."

"You are not dying. Don't cry, baby. I hate when you cry and I can't hold you."

"Lance, the plane is on fire and breaking apart. Promise me you will give someone else the chance to love you. Promise me that," I beg through tears.

"Lisa, I will only love you the rest of my life. Now, Will. You. Marry. Me?"

"Lance…I'm scared." I begin to pray, in my mind, "God please help us. Your will be done. I want to live, but your will be done for all of us." The three of us continue chanting, "Brace, Prepare, Brace."

"Lisa, baby, my heart is shredding. I want so badly to hold and protect you. Talk to me. You mentioned there was something else earlier, what did you want to tell me?"

"Lance, I…"

Turbulent Passion

Before I'm able to continue Lance screams, "I see your plane. You are going to be fine, Lisa. Do you hear me? You. Are. Going. To. Be. Fine. I will catch you. I promise…always. Now marry me, Lisa."

The plane is banking too far, *oh dear Lord, are we going to flip?* I hear screeching metal as I unwittingly exclaim, "Lance…Oh my…God Save Us!"

The last thing I hear as the plane slams into the ground erupting into a fireball is Lance's voice screaming, "L…I…S…A…!"

***

Continue Lisa and Lance's journey in *Burning Desire*

G.L. Ross

Thank you for reading *Turbulent Passion;* I hope you fell in love with Lance & Lisa. As a single mom I never have "free" time, but I always find time at the end of the day to curl up in bed with a book. Whether reading or writing, books are a wonderful journey, escape, and adventure.

I am a proud, sixth generation, native Texan. Being a true Southern Belle, I've always dreamt of the "happily ever after," the prince riding in on the white horse sweeping me off my feet. I haven't found "Prince Charming" – yet (always an optimist) – but I find him every time I discover my characters "happily ever after" endings.

My motto in life is to "always find the good," in every person and situation. Whether through laughter, prayer, or a glass of wine or vodka, I always find the good in life and share my sense of humor, love, and adventure in my stories.

Discover a passion of mine R.O.S.S. (Reach Out for Sound Support) on Facebook or visit my website www.GLRoss.com; it's time to put an end to bullying, by teaching acceptance.

Facebook: G.L. Ross, Author

Email: GayleLRoss@gmail.com

Twitter: @GayleL4

Turbulent Passion

Made in the USA
Charleston, SC
02 March 2014